# SIDECHICK BLUES  -THE PLOT

## By Nikida Bellezza

**Story by Nikida Bellezza**

**Edited by Dan Owens**

**Dedications: I thank God for this uncontrollable passion for writing, and I pray that it will always remain as such. I would like to thank my sister, Nicole Harris who gave me my first hood book to read, turning me out on the culture. To my family who have always been my rock.. and hard place, thank you forever for the love and support. I would also like to thank the folks who have been supporting me since I first started on this journey! Thank you for all of the re-posts on FB, IG and Twitter! I am grateful to every reader, and for every review that I have received! Thank you for taking the time to check me out!**

**-Nikida**

## Prologue

### Deytwon

The police escort signaled for the traffic to hold off, while I bucked a u-turn and parked next to one of the meters directly in front of the MLK Library in NW DC. Once I was parked I killed the engine. I glanced up in my rear review mirror in time to see Marcus speed forward, hit the breaks, switch gears and snap backwards into a parking space a few feet behind me. The police officers' whistle fell from his lips in shock as he watched Marcus park his car. To an outsider, Marcus seemed reckless and wild, but in reality, he was always in control. Nearly everything he did was a showboat for the folks he knew were watching. There was nothing low key about him, he thrived off attention.

I stepped out of my car and walked over to the officer who still seemed a bit shaken up behind what he just saw. He looked on as Marcus stepped out of his car and slipped on a pair of dark shades after admiring himself in the tints. Marcus then raised his hand to set the alarm on his car which sounded like a jail cell being slammed closed, followed by the sound of the guy from the Five Heartbeats whimpering '9-5.' I always got a chuckle out of his personal alarm, because only his ass could've come up with something like that.

"Thank you for your services today, Officer." I said extending my hand towards the cop.

The officer looked over at me, a little more composed but still somewhat rattled. Of course all of that eased when I shook a hundred dollar bill into his hand.

"No problem sir, just glad to be of assistance to you all. My great grandfather used to tell us stories about the Big Boys and how they helped so many people. He would be so proud of me

4

right now." The officer stated humbly.

"Indeed he would." Marcus replied as he joined the conversation.

"For your trouble." He added giving the officer a handshake of his own.

"I can't accept this, I've already been given.." The officer started.

"Sure you can. You ready to do this?" Marcus said cutting the officer off then turning his attention to me.

"As ever." I replied.

## The Legend of The Big Boys

*Marcus and I are the heads of an elite brotherhood called The Big Boys. The Big Boys were started by our Great, great, great grandfathers, during slavery. The mission was to form a syndicate of men who were dedicated to help and support those who were weaker, families who were torn apart during slave trades, or falsely accused men who had been sentenced to death. The Big Boys would do whatever they could to minimize the hardships and or support the families most affected by the hardships. Our great grandfathers slave master, Norris Phipps, wasn't a cruel dictator, like many of the rest. He was forced to inherit his slaves on his fathers deathbed. If he had it his way, he would've been studying abroad living a completely different life.*

*Having slaves out of spite gave Norris a lackadaisical attitude towards his duties as a master. In fact, he was so laid back as a master, he'd often receive death threats from neighboring masters who feared he may one day set his slaves free. Especially when rumors spread about his lack of discipline toward his slaves. Not that his troop of slaves needed discipline, they all worked hard for him, appreciating that he was nothing like the rest.*

*Without the masters knee in their back, the Big Boys were able to function and thrive in such a way that allowed them to grow in numbers. They helped all that they could, and supported the families of those they could not.*

*The group was founded by three men, whose last names were Powers, Jones and Richards. However years later the son of Powers would "mysteriously" step down after his death, and would never be heard from again.*

*During early years of the Big Boy movement, their power only came in the form of acceptance. However, all of that would change one night when a group neighboring masters had*

6

*decided to make good on their death threats.*

*The trio were accompanying their Norris on a journey to trade in cotton. They traveled late into the night and were just about ready to set up camp when suddenly out of nowhere they were attacked by hooded assailants. The Big Boy leaders sprung into action to defend themselves as well as their less than valiant master. Once the men were able to fight the attackers off, killing three of them, the rest fled and they were able to escape unscathed.*

*The Norris was so moved by the way the men risked their lives to defend him. When he got home that night, he wrote up a Will that would leave the men with one gold mine and two diamond mines in Africa. The mines were just a few of the many that the master's family had maintained ownership over. Knowing that his slaves could not read, and that the Will would likely be destroyed if it got into the wrong hands, the master had a copy of the Will drawn up and gave it to Powers on his deathbed in 1864. After the death of Norris Philips his cousin Randolph Philips the 3rd took over as master, and the slaves endured the worst year of their lives, until they were officially emancipated on December 6th, 1865.*

*Cecil Powers, not being able to read was ignorant as to what was on the paper he received for Norris, but he could tell that it was important, so he stored it in some boxes.*

*After the death Cecil Sr' wife Sadie, Cecil Jr, who the couple bore in 1850, decided that it would be best to move his father in with him. During this time Cecil Jr, and the sons of Richards and Jones were now the leaders of the Big Boys, and the former leaders were now the elders. Upon cleaning out his father's closet, Cecil Jr stumbled across the Will tucked deeply into a corner of an old wooden box. He damn near fainted when he saw what it declared. After that he called an emergency leadership meeting where he presented the Will to the leaders and elders, and together they fought for fifteen years to get what was owed to them. It was then that the Big Boys became a*

7

*power entity, and soon enough, a force to be reckoned with.*

"So which one of these ladies you think is Angel?" Marcus asked as we took seats at an empty table. We had just entered the library where we were told that Angel worked.

I scanned the room looking for the young woman in the picture that Marcus and I secured from the private detective. Normally we didn't work projects together, but this one was important, we had reason to believe that Angel is the great great great granddaughter of Cecil Powers, Leader and founder of the Big Boys.

Since Cecil Powers Jr's abandonment fifty years ago, The Big Boys have only held two leaders, which made our leadership trio one short.

"It says she's an aid, maybe she's helping someone." I replied as I continued to scan the room.

"Man, do you know how proud of us the elders would be if we brought her back. We'd be given high honors." Marcus said nodding his head as a sick smile crept his face. I loved Marcus like a brother, but his quest for power concerned me.

At the young age of 27, Marcus and I had more power than the president. It's not hard to understand how having such power can go to ones head, but my man Marcus was in a league of his own with it.

I never tried to talk sense into him, because he was my equal, and my words would only present a challenge to him, which was strictly forbidden. So I let him live and kept my distance with the exception of when power moves called us to unite.

"There she go." Marcus said with a tap to my shoulder.

I looked up to see the most beautiful woman I had ever seen in my entire life, and that was saying something seeing as though I have traveled the world.

Angel's name was so befitting of her, she looked like a chocolate Angel. Her complexion was a soft, smooth version of chocolate brown. She stood at about 5'4, with a medium build. She had the type of body that a man couldn't help but pay attention to. Full breast that were snuggled up under her form fitting sweater, and round hips that stretched the capacity of her jean skirt. Shawty was *badd*.  Her body instantly had me on swole and I've never met a woman who could do that to me!

She wore her hair in a bun with a part on the side. Her light brown eyes were giving the Sun some go (competition) as it seemed to jealously beam on her through the windows.

She smiled at what appeared to be the advances of a guy that she was giving books to. Her smile was very sexy, and it complimented her already beautiful face.

"Damn, she badd." Marcus said interrupting my gaze.

"She's gorgeous. I've been all over the world and my future wife has been in Washington, DC this whole time?" I said more to myself

I could feel Marcus turn to look at me, then he looked back at her.

"Hmm." he sort of hummed to himself.

She giggled before walking away from the guy that she had been helping. He didn't seem to want her to go though and so he decided to follow her.

"Lets move." I said as I stood to my feet. My mind wasn't even on the plan anymore, rather it was on making Angel my wife.

"Nah, hold it. What are we supposed to say to her? If we spring this on her she'll think we're crazy." Marcus said now sharing second thoughts that he never previously expressed having.

9

"We engage her in conversation, then go from there." I replied. To me it was simple, though again, because my mind had become sidetracked, my conversation with Angel would've been a little different now.

"Two men wearing suits approaching her? She's going to think we're feds. This isn't the way." Marcus said shaking his head.

"yeah? What Fed you know wear 100 thousand dollar suites and forty thousand dollar watches?" I asked wondering what was really going on with his change of heart.

I knew Marcus, something was up. If we brought her to the Elders today, we would be honored, which is something Marcus lived for, so why was he stalling now?

"Deytwon, I don't know man, something just doesn't feel right. We should leave." He said as his entire tone and body language seemed to deflate.

I gave him a very peculiar look. His sudden apprehension raised a flag in my mind. However, instead of pressing him, I decided to allow things to unfold by themselves. No matter how hard a person tries to hide the truth, it always had a way of getting out.

I gave Angel one last glance, and noticed that she was laughing at something the guy was telling her, seconds before a stern looking woman approached them to break it up. I suppose, to remind her that she was at work.

"One day soon baby girl, one day soon.." I said just as Marcus tapped my arm.

"Come on man, let's jet to New York and grab something to eat before we split up." Marcus suggested.

"Bet." I replied as I headed towards the door.

## Marcus

"Yeah man, just let me run to the bathroom right quick and we can be out." I said to Deytwon as we headed for the door.

"Aright man, don't drown nigga, I got other shit to do." Deytwon said looking at his watch.

"Piss n shake man, in and out."I said with a slap to his back.

Once he was out of sight I looked over at Angel to see if she was still talking with that clown ass nigga who wouldn't leave her alone. Good thing for him she wasn't. Now she was collecting books off the table and placing them in a cart. I walked over to her and started helping her.

Initially the plan was to meet her and present her with her birthright, while I cooked up other plans to snatch it all away behind the scenes. But I never counted on her being beautiful enough for Deytwon to fall in love with her on sight. His affections for her threw a serious wrench in my plans, and for the simple fact that my man has never been in love, I knew that he would go hard for her. I had to cut him off at the pass, while he was my man a hundred grand, I couldn't let him spoil my plans for Angel. There was no way that I could allow her to take her seat, and especially not as his wife.

"How you doing?" I asked as I handed her a book.

"I'm good, thank you." She said taking the book and placing it in the cart.

"So what's ya name?" I asked taking up more books.

"Angel." She replied looking at me for the first time. Her soft brown eyes almost had my attention. When she noticed me staring, a smile widened her soft thick lips and she cocked her head to the side.

"Nice to meet you Angel, I'm Marcus. So look, I gotta get out of here, but before I do, I got two questions for you. You think you can answer them for me?" I asked.

"I'll try" She replied with a flirtatious smile.

"Cool, do you have a man, and can I call you?" I asked. She bust out laughing.

"But if I say I have a man, wouldn't that cancel that second question out?" She asked

"That first question was a lead in. I really don't care how you answer that one." I said.

"But, if I have a man, that would make the second answer *no,* anyway, right." She said with a shrug.

"Would it?" I asked.

"I would think so." She replied with a chuckle

"You looking for me to convince you?" I asked.

"No." She replied with a smile

"So you already know what you want to do?" I asked.

"yeah." She said nodding her head.

I took out my phone and pulled up add contacts before handing it to her.

"Oh my gawd, is this what I said I wanted to do?" She asked with a laugh.

"We both know it is, why fight it? I wont tell if you don't." I said with a wink.

"I don't know if you're cocky or just sure of yourself." She said holding my phone.

"Go 'head and put your number in there and find out." I said nodding my head towards my phone.

"OK Marcus." She said before adding her info.

"Aright shawty, I'll get at you before the weeks out. Maybe next time I see you I'll get to taste them lips." I said testing her to see if she'd go for it.

"Is *that* what you wanna do?" she asked as though she were calling me out.

"Trust me, you wont complain or regret it. I holla." I said turning to leave before she could respond.

When I got outside I saw Deytwon in his Cadillac sitting in front of the building talking on his cell. I gave him a head nod before I walked over to get inside my Jaguar. On my signal, the officer from early pulled out to stop traffic so that Deytwon and I could pull off.

Sidechick Blues The Plot by Nikida Bellezza

## Chapter 1

*(Three months later..)*

### Marcus

*'Damn, thought this bitch would never shut the fuck up. A nigga gotta fake sleep to get her to close her mouth.'* I thought to myself as I lay in bed with my eyes closed. After a few hours of fuckin and smoking I just needed a lil break from shawty. She was cool, but she nagged the shit out of me, yapping about nothing but her boring ass life. I played It cool because I needed to keep her on my line, but at the same time, a nigga can only take so much.

I gradually allowed my eyes to close as she went on talking about her job, and how they be blowing her, and blah blah blah. *"Yeah yeah, slim, yeah yeah."* was what was on my mind to say, but in reality, I didn't want to argue before letting her suck me off. Besides that, arguments were my outro, so I used them wisely.

I think I did unintentionally doze off though, eventually. The bed was comfortable as shit, that's why I loved coming to The Embassy Suite, their beds were the business, and their pillows, man what? I could sleep all day with no problem. The sleep was just starting to get good when I felt her hand stroking my dick.

Suddenly my dick got hard and woke all the rest of me up. Her soft hands slowly drifting up and down on my shaft, stretching open as my dick grew inside them. Yeah, I was all the way up now.

I felt her hair trickle down my stomach as she moved towards my lower half, her tongue bounced off my skin on its way to home plate. She knew how to sice a nigga, that's for sure, but another second of teasing, I would've put my shit in her mouth my damn self. Then, that moment when you feel her warm, wet, soft mouth drape over your dick...

14

"Mmmm..." I moaned ready to let her know that I was awake.

*****

## Angel

There was nothing at all in my life that felt as good as the moments I shared with Marcus. No matter how bad my day was going, a text or visit from him would turn things around one hundred and eighty degrees. He was my good feeling, my 'looking forward to' activity, my reason, and I was satisfied being whatever I could be to him. The boy had me wide open, and he knew it and I didn't even give a damn.

We had been chilling in a hotel room for most of the day. Hotels were the only place that we could meet up and be alone uninterrupted. From the moment we stepped into the door, I would cut my phone off and toss it to the side. Our moments together were often far and few between so I wanted to be sure that we gave one another every second that we had together.

After a couple hours of teasing, back breaking, orgasm shaking sex, I lay on his chest with my arms wrapped around his body. I enjoyed the way his heartbeat would pulsate against my own. It was like listening to a soft drummers beat. The room was filled with a mixture of his cologne and the dro we had been smoking. He was fast asleep with one hand rested on my ass and the other between my breast. I loved when he had free afternoons because they were spent with me, or so I believed. Marcus had long ago become my crack and I damn sure needed my fix way too often.

I gazed up at his face and watched him breathe in deeply as he enjoyed his sleep. He looked so peaceful and handsome.

"Damn nigga, the fuck did you do to me?" I asked softly as I smoothed my thumb along his sexy lips, which only served to make me horny all over again, but I knew the remedy for that. I stretched my hand under the blanket until I reached his thick ass dick. Even on soft the man was large, and I loved it!

I dragged my fingers up and down his shaft until I got a rise, then I took it into my mouth and went to work. Seconds later he stirred awake and grabbed the back if my head.

"Damn shawty, you know how to wake a mufucka up out his sleep, shit." He said.

"Mmhmm." I hummed on his dick.

"You gonna swallow that for me?" He asked.

"Don't I always?" I asked never relieving my mouth of him.

"That's my girl" he said as he leaned his head back into the pillow.

After I sucked the life out of him I slid up and straddled him while running my hands all over his sexy rippling chest.

"Nah shawty, get the fuck down, you know I ain't wit this." He said with his eyes still closed.

"Please daddy, just put the head in." I moaned as I bumped my clit against his head. He sat up and pushed me off of him.

"I fuckin hate when you do that shit!" He exclaimed as I fell onto the bed.

"Really all that though?!" I yelled as I stood up beside the bed.

"The fuck you don't understand Angel? I only fuck one woman raw and that's my wife. Is your fuckin name Mrs. Jones? Nah, aright then, it ain't you!" He exclaimed as he stepped into his jeans.

"You kill me, you fuckin act like I got something, like I'm a dirty bitch out here!" I shouted throwing his shirt at him.

16

"I don't give a fuck if you as clean as Howard Hughes bedroom, you ain't my fuckin wife, this raw dick ain't yours!" He exclaimed.

"Who the fuck is Howard Hughes?" I asked confused. He looked up at me squinting his eyes like he was confused by my ignorance as he continued to buckle his belt.

Giving no reply at all, he shook his head and pulled his shirt over his head just as Dedicated by R Kelly began to play on his phone.

"Look slim, I know you mad, but don't say shit, aright." He said to me as I watched the name 'The Wife' flash across the phone. I shook my head and started putting my clothes on.

"What's up baby girl?" He asked before he walked away.

After I got dressed I sat on the edge of the bed and cried. I was tired of being his lil secret, although I knew what it was from jump. It was all good before my feelings got involved, and now my common sense had me all fucked up over this.

"Fuck wrong with you now?" He asked as he walked back into the room after his ten minute conversation.

"Why in the fuck are you always talking' to me like I'm some nigga? You ain't got no more respect for me than that?" I exclaimed starting a fight to get my frustrations out.

"Is you for real? You really coming' at me wit all this fuckin heat cause I won't stick my dick up in you raw? Shawty, tell me this ain't what this shit is all about. Please." He said upset.

"We been knowing' each other for a minute and we been fuckin for months, but you treat me like shit. I know I ain't the wife, but I ain't just no anything ass bitch either, nigga! You keep coming' back for a reason! And we do more than fuck! We go out, we talk, we hang..." I started to go on but he cut me short.

"*And*?" He asked interrupting me.

"I don't mean shit to you, Marcus?" I asked softer, ready for him to give it to me straight.

He sighed and shook his head

"I ain't got time for this shit joe, you need a ride or what 'cause I bout to roll." He said totally dismissing me.

"Fuck you!" I exclaimed grabbing my coat and walking out the door.

"I have a fuckin' wife, the fuck you want me to do? What is it that you asking me?" He asked following me out of the room.

"You don't feel nothing' for me?" I asked after turning around to face him.

"I'm saying', you cool, I care about you.. But I love her" He replied.

"So then why are you fucking me?" I asked with my hands on my hips. He just looked at me and shook his head.

"Is that a question, or you trying to make a deal?" He asked.

"You can't take shit serious. I don't even know what the fuck I'm even doing' messing' around with you." I said shaking my head frustrated as hell.

"Getting' the best fuckin' dick of your life, from a nigga that can't be all about you, in a situation that you walked into wit' your eyes wide open. Take the shit, or leave the shit. I'm not holding' you hostage. I like fuckin' you too, but my life ain't wrapped up in this shit, so why is yours?" He asked.

"You are so cold." I said shaking my head.

"No I'm not. I'm real. Big difference, lets roll." He said before walking passed me. I shook my head and followed him to the elevator. The fuck was I going to do, he was right, my pussy made the call and he was it, until my mind could convince me otherwise.

****

## Chapter 2

### Marcus

"Again bitch? damn." I said to myself after seeing that it was Angel texting me. She had texted me every two days, since our argument at the hotel. All that fight she had about how I took her for granted was being liquidated. Now she missed me and hoped I wasn't mad. Beautiful as she was, she was a silly bitch.

I figured I'd let her go a lil while without me. Let her miss me so that when I came back she'd be ready to do all the shit I love, and anything I wanted her to out of fear of losing me again.

My conscience was flexible, it allowed me to make necessary moves to get what and where I wanted. So dogging' Angel out wasn't shit to me. She was a pawn in my plan to keep her away from Deytwon. I loved him like a brother but allowing them two to hook up and outshine me wasn't even about to be the plan. Fuck what you heard.

And just in case me slutting her ass out isn't enough to change his mind, I made sure to fuck her up from the inside out. Get her emotionally hooked, controlling her mind, once I had that the rest was cake.  A cruddy nigga yes, bow to another nigga, never.

Seeing how I was horny and it had been a week since I got some of her good suck, I figured it was time to take Angel off the shelf. My wife had some bomb ass pussy, but she didn't have Angels skill set, and I was in need of a re-up.

I was on my way to pull a pop up on her. I knew she was home because she didn't do anything but wait around for me. And after that text I got, I knew she'd be ready to give it up. When I got to her house I saw her crush a cigarette under her foot and was about to turn around until I called out to her

19

"**Damn shawty, you bad as shit, what's your name?**" I asked. She started shining like a light bulb when she saw me.

*'yeah, I got that ass like shit.'* I thought to myself with a chuckle as she approached my car.

### Angel

It had been a week since I last spoke with Marcus. No text, no call, he didn't even update his FB or IG. But his wife did. I was her friend on facebook under an assumed name and her IG was public, so it wasn't hard to spy on her there. Apparently, out of the goodness of his heart, he purchased her a Chanel bracelet and necklace, and flew her to New York to have dinner at some Italian restaurant, as he knew Italian was her favorite food.

"Damn bitch, brag much?" I said as I closed the facebook app on my phone. I couldn't take it anymore, hurt and anger consumed me, now more so because I hadn't heard from him.

If she deserved all that, then why was he fuckin me.

*'Obviously she ain't putting it down like I do or he wouldn't stray.'* I thought to myself as I tossed my phone somewhere in the corner behind my bed.

"Eew I HATE HIM!" I shouted before leaving my room.

"You hate who?" Asked Salisha, my roommate and best friend.

"It don't even matter, I'm done with the shit." I answered not really wanting to discuss it with her morally conscious ass. I didn't need nobody to tell me how stupid I was. I needed somebody to tell me how to get and keep his ass.

"Girl, I swear if you talking' 'bout Marcus we goin' fight." She said as I grabbed my cigarettes from the table.

"Can you do me a favor though?" I asked after retrieving a cigarette from the pack and taking out my lighter.

"What's up?" She asked ignorantly walking into my sarcastic trap.

"Mind ya business. If I don't ask you shit, don't tell me shit." I said before heading

21

towards the door.

"Don't take your anger out on me just cause you living a life your soul can't handle!" She called behind me.

I waved my middle finger at her before I left the apartment.

"Sup Ange." Asked my neighbor Rick who had already been outside smoking a black.

"Ain't shit, what's up?" I asked back as I lit my cigarette.

"Shit, you heard some niggas shot up Q's apartment the other night?" He asked.

"Nah, when that happen?" I asked shocked.

"Like two nights ago, you must not'a been home, cause them niggas was popping' thee fuck off, they was getting' it. I know Q a dirty nigga but damn." Rick said shaking his head

"Damn, did they get him though?" I asked before taking pull of my cigarette

"Nah, he wasn't even home, and ain't been back either." He replied.

"Shiiiit, would you?" I asked with a chuckle.

"Fuck no, but I don't get my hands dirty like that either, so its all wins for me." He said with a chuckle of his own.

"True, but it don't even always take that, a nigga could just want what you got, and that would be enough to get you." I said thinking about Marcus.

"True shit, aright shawty, let me get back up in here before Terina cuss me the fuck out. The baby don't be letting' her get no kinda sleep." He said as he put his black out against the building.

"The life of new parents huh?" I asked.

"You better know it, aright young." Rick said dapping me up before he walked off.

I took a seat on my stoop and continued smoking as my mind began to drift towards thoughts of Marcus.

I missed the shit out of him, his smell, his touch, his laugh, his walk, his talk, how he eat, how he sleep. Even arguing with him was worth it.

"Damn, how I let this nigga get to me like this?" I often found myself asking this question, but never having an answer for it.

After smoking it down to a butt, I dropped my cigarette and crushed it under my feet just as I heard a car pull up.

"Damn shawty, you bad as shit, what's your name?" I heard Marcus' voice ask. I looked up to see Marcus sitting in his Cadillac in front of my building.

Before I could stop it my face beamed with sheer delight. Everything inside me came alive at the sight of him.

"Hey you." I said attempting to play down my excitement, but it was too late, the secret had already been told as it was written all over my face.

"What's up slim, you trying to take a ride wit me real quick?" He asked as I approached his car.

'*Hell yeah!*' Everything inside me shouted.

"Where?" I asked coolly still trying to play down my feelings.

"Does it matter? Ain't you always good when you wit me?" He asked.

I smiled and shook my head as I got into his car.

"I'm still mad at you though." I said.

"Join the club, they meet on Tuesdays." He replied as he punched hard on the gas tossing us back onto the seats hard.

"Why you ain't hit me all week though?" I asked calling myself giving up attitude, in reality I wasn't mad anymore, but I was trying to save face. Let him know I don't approve or tolerate how he carried me over the last week.

"For real shawty, this what we going' do on our first day getting' back at each other?" He asked.

"I just wanna know why I had to pull out my dildo for the first time in months." I said calmer attempting to not upset him.

"I'm saying, we can't be up under each other all the time. I gotta let you miss me sometimes, can't let you get too used to it, that's how shit get boring', feel me?" He said as he rubbed my thigh.

"Truue." I replied smiling, giving in to what I KNEW was pure bullshit. The truth was, the moment he pulled up at my place I forgave him. I just wanted to be with him, and now, I was.

"So what's up, you hungry?" He asked.

"yeah." I answered.

"Bet, we going' ride out Va, sit, eat, kick it, then slide to the hotel, cool?" He said.

"That works." I was all too happy to be in his presence again.

"Damn I missed the FUCK outta that dick! I shouted as he passed me the jay that we'd been sending back and forth.

"I know you did, I heard that kitty calling' me from all the way across town." He replied as he got out of bed and put his boxers back on.

"Where you going?" I asked blowing smoke from my mouth as I talked. He looked over at me confused.

"Damn slim, can I piss?" He asked heading towards the bathroom.

"My bad, I just ain't get a chance to bob that joint, I ain't ready to leave." I said cleaning it up.

"yeah, you know I ain't turning' down no head, not yo head skills, no way." He said before walking into the bathroom. I shook my head and continued to hit the jay.

*'Damn, gotta stop acting pressed. that's what kept his ass away for a week the last time.'* I thought to myself

"Damn shawty, you going' hit that to yourself or what?" He asked once he returned from the bathroom.

"My bad, you taking' all long, what was I supposed to do, just hold it and smell it?" I asked with a chuckle as I handed it to him.

"True. So what's good, you need a lil something' or you straight?" He asked sitting in the edge of the bed.

"I always need money, I ain't making' shit working' at Shoppers." I complained as I took back the jay. He took up his pants and went into his pocket to pull out a wad of money that was secured in a silver clip.

"So why you work there then? What I tell you, if shit ain't helping' you, it's hurting' you." He said as he pulled four one hundred dollar bills out of a clip and tossed them at me.

"Where I'm supposed to work, ain't nobody hiring." I said taking the money and slipping it into my pocket.

"yeah, ain't nobody hiring where you choose to look, nah." He said taking the jay from me then walking away with it. He grabbed his phone off the coffee table and sat on the couch.

"So I'm bout to get a lecture now?" I asked resting up on my knees

"Nah, it's your life, you gotta live it for you, not me. You gotta be comfortable. I'm good."

He said going through his phone.

"How you on your phone when you supposed to be getting' at me? You cheating' me out of my Marcus time!" I exclaimed with my hands on my hips

"Oh yeah?" He asked finally looking up and over at me.

"Yeah nigga!" I said copping a fake attitude but with a smile happy to see that I had his attention.

"I hear you talking', but fuck you going' do 'bout it, my attention span is short. If you want my attention, you gotta show me why you deserve it" He said.

I stood up and did my sexy walk across the room. When I got to him, I got on my knees and opened his legs.

"Oh yeah?" I asked softly tilting my neck to express more fake attitude

"No doubt." He replied.

"Mmmhmm." I hummed before kissing my way down his thigh. When I got to his boxers, I licked the head through the opening, then I pulled them down and went to work on his dick.

"So when i'ma' see you again?" I asked as we pulled up to my apartment.

"I don't know, let's wing it like we do now." He said.

"yeah aright, whatever." I said sucking my teeth. I hopped out of the car and marched up to my building.

"What's the problem now?" He called behind me.

"Nothing, you don't give a fuck no way." I yelled back as I stomped up the steps.

"Help me out with something'." I heard him say as he slammed his door close.

I turned around to face him with my arms folded and my head cocked ready to give him a

Sidechick Blues The Plot by Nikida Bellezza

full blast of my attitude.

"Do you know I'm married?" He asked

"yeah but.." I started but he put a finger up telling me to wait.

"Do you know that I love and am not leaving my wife for shit?" He asked.

"You said that, but." I started but was stopped again.

"So then you know that at this point, I'm giving you what I can. Go 'head and tell me it's not enough, and I'll leave you alone right now." He said with a careless shrug.

"I just be missing' you Marcus, you don't get that?" I asked losing the heat that fueled my frustration at the thought of losing him.

"Am I dying?" He asked.

"No." I said.

"Right, what you think you not going' ever see me again?" He asked as he touched my arm.

"It be feeling' like that sometimes." I replied.

"But I always come back to you, don't I?" He asked.

"Yes, you do." I said putting my arms around him.

"Aright then, so stop fussing' at me for nothing', aright." He said pulling back.

"OK, I'm out my feelings." I smiled just as he kissed me on the side of my neck, which is what he did instead of kissing my lips.

"So that four going' hold you til I see you or you need more?" He asked referring to the money he had given me.

"I'm straight." I replied as I reasoned that he'd come back sooner.

"Bet, aright shawty, I'll get up wit'cha' sometime, sometime. Keep that thang tight and wet." He said with a slap to my ass before heading back to his car.

"Aright sexy." I said before turning to head up to my apartment.

It wasn't until I got to my door that I realized I had left my keys and phone inside. I hated waking Salisha up to open the door for me, she always had something self-righteous to say. She was far from a saint but she seemed to pride herself on being less of a sinner than me.

"Damn you know what time it is? Where you been? I been blowing up your phone like shit" Salisha went in on me after opening the door.

"Lisha, I know you mad for being woke up, but all that shit you doing', I don't need right now, aright." I said as I walked by her.

"You're welcome bitch!" She said letting the door close.

"Thank you, I appreciate you letting me in, OKAY" I said turning around to face her.

"yeah whatever, I want details tomorrow tramp!" She said before going into her room. I laughed and headed to my own room to crash.

****

## Chapter 3

### Deytwon

It had been months since Marcus and I saw Angel for the first time up at the MLK Library. I thought about her everyday, but oddly enough, Marcus and I never spoke on it again.

I still couldn't help but be curious as to why Marcus just dropped it like it was nothing, when he was the one who was most excited about finding her and bringing her to the elders in the first place. I didn't think too much on it though, but Angel did stay on my mind.

There was something about her that made something inside me come alive. She had become an addiction for whatever this life force inside me was. It wanted her, and it wanted her badly.

After going back to the library to check for her on my own, I discovered that she was no longer working there. An overly friendly ex co-worker of hers told me that she had been working at Shoppers for a few months now. I got the address and decided to go pay her a visit.

I didn't know what I wanted to say, I only knew that I wanted to say something. To have her eyes looking at me. To hear her voice, and watch her smile. I had to feed this monster that wanted this woman so badly.

When I pulled up to shoppers, I parked my truck and headed inside. I had no game or strategy, I was just gonna play it by ear. For the first time in my life, I was approaching a woman with good intentions, beyond a night of sheer ecstasy, breakfast and goodbye flowers. No, this woman here had me in a bad way. I've never been one to believe in love at first sight, and used to clown the whole concept. Now I was playing the fool, lead like a fool on a fools journey, just hoping for the best.

When I got inside the store I walked around trying to be inconspicuous and I looked through the aisle for this woman, whom I had already deemed to be my future wife.

I could feel my heart panting as I got closer to the back of the store. I didn't know if I was getting closer to her energy, or if I was preparing to be disappointed by trying to catch her on her day off.

Finally, I came to an aisle where I saw a woman with Angel's same build. She wore her hair combed back in a low ponytail and was dressed in her work shirt and a pair of jeans. She was bobbing her head to some music playing through her headphones as she stocked the shelves. Even dressed this way, she was still the most beautiful woman I had ever seen in my life.

I took a deep breath and slowly began my descent down the aisle to approach her and accept my fate.

"How you doing? I asked to get her attention...

## Angel

The next morning I woke up, made a bowl of cereal and headed out to work. It was my early day so I was up and out before Salisha woke up. When I got to work I clocked in and went straight for the re-shop first.

"Excuse me hun, what aisle is the bacon on?" A woman asked me as she placed her toddler son in the cart.

"Aisle seven, all the way down on the other end." I replied.

"Aright." She said before walking away.

I shook my head and turned around to continue working. Once the re-shop was done I went to the back to grab a pallet of food that needed to be stocked and ran into my co-worker Chris.

"Whats good my AaaaaaaannGEL?" Chris sang when he saw me.

"Whats up?" I asked with a laugh as I jacked the pallet up.

"Ain't shit, so they got you in the morning' today huh?" He asked

"yeah, and I ain't mad about it. Get in, get out." I replied

"No doubt, well aright baby girl, i'ma' holla at you at lunch, you going' at twelve today?" He asked.

"Something like that. Why, you treating'?" I asked before I got to the door.

"I can, but its going' be something' like McDonald's." He said.

"That's a bet." I said before leaving out.

"There you go, I been looking' for you!" My coworker My'esha said as she approached me.

"What's up Eash." I said as I dragged the pallet down the aisle.

"So you know I let Tyrone come through last night right?" She asked in a hushed tone.

"Get the fuck outta here!" I exclaimed as I dropped the pallet jack on the floor.

"No mu'fuckin' lie. You know he been asking' me what's up for a minute. So yesterday I told him come by my place. He was like cool. We was chilling', talking', watching' movies, and he had brought some four twenty.." She said referring to weed.

"You watched him roll though, right?" I asked interrupting her.

"Of course, I helped him roll, shit. I don't fuck around with the pre wraps. But anyway, we hit it, then we started kissing', touching', next thing I know I'm scratching' my name in this nigga back." She said excited.

"I know that shit was good." I said shaking my head. Tyrone was fine as hell and even sexier than that. I could tell just off how he walk that he had a big dick and a mean stroke.

"Slim, we fucked like eight times. He ended up spending the night, then we fucked again this morning. He dropped me off like a hour ago." She said.

"Damn, that's what's up." I replied as I grabbed the jack to pull the the pallet towards the aisle.

"Tell me about it. Well I just wanted to tell you that, let me get up in this cash office, I holla." She said

"Aright trick" I replied as I continued towards the aisle.

When I got to the front of the aisle, I quickly stuffed an earphone in my ear and turned the music up. I knew it was going to take a heavy dose of GoGo to help me get through this day. I was a big R.E. and JY fan, though most people my age liked Back and TCB. It was just in me too strong to rock with the old head bands.

32

With the music blasting in my ear, I was able to finish stocking the right side of the aisle within thirty minutes, so I moved over to the other side and got busy.

"How you doing?" I heard a male voice ask from behind while I cut open boxes.

"Hey." I said turning around to see a very handsome man behind me. He was light brown with a low cut and shape up and a sexy goatee. He stood about six two and had a medium build, definitely my type of guy.

"Can you tell me where the lotion is, a nigga tired of walking around ashy, looking' like a box of powdered donuts got the best of me an' shit." He said jokingly

"I didn't know light skin people got ashy " I replied after laughing at him.

"Nah we do, the shit just look like dandruff on us though." He said.

"Really?" I replied laughing a little harder.

"I'm glad I can make you laugh at my flaws, Angel." He said looking at my name tag.

"I mean how you talk about them, I figure you must laugh too." I replied still chuckling.

"Its cool, my name Deytwon. Nice to meet you." He said as he stuck his hand out for me to shake.

"Angel." I replied forgetting that he already knew.

"No bullshit? 'Cause I ain't just say that." He said raising an eyebrow.

"My bad, force of habit when somebody tell me they name." I said still giggling.

"Nah, you good, you get a pass for being beautiful. So look, before I combust into a pile of ash, what nigga I gotta knock out to get your number?" He asked.

"Wow, for real? I look like I'd be with a nigga that can't throw?" I asked with my hand on my hips.

"He might can throw, but he ain't seeing' me, not many niggas out here can." He replied

**very sure of himself.**

"Damn, cocky much?" I asked.

"Very much, but I'm too quick for most niggas, and for the rest, I'm too strong." He explained.

"So then why you single, what chick don't want a man like that?" I asked curious.

"I don't make time for game players, only game changers. I just haven't met one yet, and I'm not about to sacrifice" He said.

"I feel that." I replied

"So can I call you?" He asked.

"How do you know that *I'm* not a game player though?" I asked flirting

"I don't." He replied with a shrug

"But you want to call me?" I asked.

"Nothing' beats a failure but a try." He said.

"My grandmother used to say that." I replied.

"Cause grandma knew." He said.

"Knew what?" I asked.

"I don't know, are you side stepping my request for a reason?" He asked

"I'm just not in that place right now, I'm in a situation and I'm really trying to deal with it." I said not trying to give up too many details about my relationship with Marcus

"I can dig it, but let me ask you a question." He said.

"Go head." I said.

"Are you happy?" He asked.

"I'm good." I replied

"Nah, you not happy. When a woman is happy she smiles and have that distant look in her eyes when she talks about her man, and she damn sure don't reply 'I'm good.' But I tell you what, I'm not going' press you. Take my card, if you ever get tired of just being' *good*, hit me up." He said taking his card out of his wallet.

"Deytwon Richards, Computer Graphics and web design. IT specialist. This is what you do?" I asked.

"Nah, see, I just like making cards with my name and different things I wish I could do." He said

I burst out laughing at him.

"This is one of the things I do." He said with a chuckle.

"One of the things?" I asked

"Yes ma'am, I am a man of many talents." He said.

"Gotcha." I replied.

"Nice meeting you Angel " He said

"You too." I replied before he walked off.

"OH MY GAWD GIRL, who in the fuck was THAT?" My coworker Dasia asked as she ran into me.

"Damn girl, can he get out the fuckin aisle?" I said trying to calm her down, even though he had already bent the corner.

"Yung, I saw his ass come in, he fine as fuckin hell! AND he driving' a black Benz truck with specialized license plates that say BB with three stars. I wonder if hes somebody important! PLEASE tell me you gave him your number!" She exclaimed.

"No, I didn't, he was cocky as shit." I said lying about the reason I didn't give him my number.

"Bitch is you crazy? He got the deed to that right to be as cocky as he wanna be! Shiiit, he can get it all day. I don't know what the fuck wrong wit' yo ass!" She said

"Bitch you geekin' like shit, why don't you go holla at him if its like that?" I asked.

"Because you don't walk up to a nigga like him, they don't trust thirsty bitches." She said.

"Yung, you lunchin like shit, bye bye, let me get back to work." I said putting my headphones back into my ears.

"Whateva." She said rolling her eyes before walking away.

### Deytwon

I stood in my restaurant feeling pleased with the progress that was made. It was transformed from a huge rundown barn into a mansion size restaurant. In fact it was the epitome of restaurants. If a nigga didn't have at lease a thousand dollars to drop comfortably, there was no need in him coming through. Not that I was shittin' on the less fortunate, but this restaurant wasn't your average. It was created for wealthy men to bring their mistresses and side chicks.

I got the idea a couple of months ago while I was dining at The Four Seasons with some business partners. A man was out on a date with a woman whom we came to know was his mistress, was busted by his wife. She of course caused a scene and the once elegant restaurant became a war zone.

Although I personally don't do the side chick thing, as it was never my style, I understood that he was just looking for a nice spot to take this chick where he could flatter her with his money. I figured that I could do him one better, I would create a location that's only for side chicks. With a smooth chill atmosphere, and the best of everything. The only requirement is, you have to pay to play.

That's how I came up with Sides, the restaurant that I was now standing in, admiring. I hired the best of the best to help put this place together. From artist, to sculptors, architects, decorators, designers, you name it, I had them in here. It all came together perfectly. All I needed now were the customers. I pulled out my cell to call Marcus, he'd get the first invite, it was only right..

<><><>

### Marcus

I sat in my lounge chair on my deck and stared up at the ceiling as I thought about the head Angel gave me last night. She really outdid herself, I almost couldn't drive her home I was so weak. She's a boss at that shit anyway, but she becomes a monster when she think she about to lose me. I'ma' have to make her think I'm always ready to dip if its gonna get me head like that.

"Damn Dey, I cheated the shit out of you on this one bruh." I said to myself with a chuckle as I felt my phone vibrate against me.

"Speaking' of the muthafuckin' devil." I said to myself as Deytwon's number flashed across the screen

"Yo." I said after pushing the button to answer.

"What's good man, so you know the restaurant is ready and open for business. The invites are out, showtime is Friday night." Deytwon said.

"This Friday?" I asked to be sure.

"No doubt." Deytwon replied.

"Aright, that's a bet. I know that shit gonna be crazy. A haven for the side chick, nigga who does that?" I said with a laugh.

"Aw man, wait til you get there, it ain't nothing like anything out here. You think you seen some shit, but you ain't seen shit yet!' Deytwon replied.

*'Nah nigga, you ain't seen shit yet. Wait til you see who I'm bringing.'* I thought to myself.

"I mean, but that's how it should be, either go hard or go home right?" I asked.

"That's my motto. But aright man, I'll shoot you the address and I'll see you there." Deytwon said.

38

**"Bet."** I said ending the call. I leaned my head back on the chair and looked up and smiled at my thoughts. I planned to bring Angel, this would definitely be a night to remember!

## Chapter 4

### Angel

While I was at work Salisha sent me a text saying that she was spending the night with her boyfriend leaving me home alone. Needless to say I was bored as shit when I got home from work. I text Marcus, letting him know that I was alone, but after ten minutes of waiting for him to reply I said fuck it. I rolled a jay and left my apartment to see if my neighbor Steve was home.

"What's good ma." He said after opening the door.

"I got treats." I said holding up the jay.

"That's what's up, come on in." He said holding the door open for me. We walked back to his bedroom where I plopped down on his beanbag chair.

"So what's good, where that faggy ass Marcus at?" He asked handing me a lighter.

"Why he gotta be all that though?" I asked after lighting the jay.

"Lets see, the nigga married an he fuckin around on his wife." He replied.

"With me." I said as I passed the jay to him.

"Right." He said before taking a hit.

"So what does that make *me*?" I asked cocking my head to the side.

"Lost." He answered with a shrug as he passed the jay back to me.

Steve didn't have any cut cards. He had no problem telling you how he felt and didn't bite his tongue for shit. He was a real as they came. I didn't always want to hear what he had to say, but I respected him for it. We become cool when I first moved in with Salisha. He helped me move my things in and somehow we got on the topic of weed and been cool every since. We never had sex and never even discussed it. I think every chick need a guy friend that's off limits for no reason at all.

"But why I'm lost cause I enjoy the niggas company and his dick?" I asked passing it back.

"Cause he will never be yours, and you know it, and I know that's gotta be fuckin wit'chu' even a lil bit." He said.

"I'm not going' lie, it is." I said taking the jay.

"So why do it?" He asked.

"'Cause I can't help myself." I replied honestly.

"You can, you just don't want to. But you got two options... you can either get it together, or wait til you ain't got no choice." He said.

"When won't I have a choice?" I asked laughing. I knew that he knew that I could handle my own.

"When he stops giving you one." Steve replied after blowing smoke from his mouth.

Steve and I hung out talking and watching movies until I fell asleep. He woke me up a few hours later.

"Shawty...shawty... wake up." I heard Steve say as he gently rocked me.

"Mmmh, what time is it?" I asked as I sat up and stretched.

"Three, I gotta go to work, come on." He said as he grabbed his keys and left the room. I stood up and followed him through his apartment and over to my apartment.

"So you good, you need me to go in and check around?" He asked as I pulled out my keys.

"Nah I'm good. I holla." I said as I slipped inside and headed straight to my room where I collapsed onto my bed and immediately went back to sleep.

I woke up the next morning to the smell of Salisha making breakfast. I crawled out of bed and immediately headed to the kitchen to steal a piece of bacon before I got dressed for work.

"What's up chick, what you doing' home? I thought you was kicking' it with Anthony?" I said as I took a couple pieces of bacon.

"He ain't have no food, so we went grocery shopping. Then we came over here so I could cook breakfast. He in the bathroom now." She said poking around at the bacon and sausage in the pan.

"Oh, so what y'all getting into today?" I asked just as Anthony came out of the bathroom.

"Probably chill, no real plans." She said.

"Damn baby, you got this whole joint smelling' like the pancake house! That's what's up, I know I picked the right one!" Anthony said as he walked over and put his arms around Salisha.

"And don't forget it!" She exclaimed.

"Aye, wussup Angel? How you been?" He asked when he noticed me.

"I be aces baby." I replied with a chuckle before I turned to leave.

I went back into my room to grab my robe, then I went into the bathroom to shower. Once I was dressed I rejoined them in the kitchen.

"Hey I made you a plate, you might have to put it in the microwave." Salisha said turning to face me as she paused from feeding Anthony.

"Ahh shit, I know what y'all bout to do. Aright I'm out!" I said with a laugh as I grabbed my plate and headed for the door.

"Whateva!" Salisha called behind me laughing before the door closed.

I sat in my car and ate, then I drove to work. When I got there I parked my car just as I heard Marcus' ring tone play on my phone.

"Hello?" I asked happily answering the phone. I was always careful to answer with caution just in case.

"Sup shawty, what's good, you miss me?" He asked.

"Always, you miss me?" I asked smiling hard as I walked towards the store.

"I'm calling you right? So what you getting' into tonight?" He asked.

"Shit, probably hit a jay and go to bed." I said feeling pathetic, I really needed a life.

"Well look, I got to ride out Moco for my man's restaurant opening' tonight, you trying to roll wit' me?" He asked.

"Hell yeah, what time?" I asked excited that he wanted me with him for that.

"I'll scoop you 'bout eight, this ain't no chill spot, I need you to be bad tonight, you got something to wear? I'm talking' classy." He said.

"Don't go there, you know I do bad, well." I said.

"yeah you do, so aright shawty, I be at your place 'bout eight." He said.

"OK see you then babes." I said before we hung up.

From that moment on I worked my entire shift in the best mood. Marcus had that magic. He could change my mood from bad to good and vice versa in a heartbeat.

While at work I called and begged my girl Karen to do my hair for me. She agreed to fit me in right after work. Not even a minute after my shift was over did I clock out and head towards my car.

<><><>

"I'm glad you got yo ass here on time because I'm booked up like shit!" Karen said when I walked into her shop.

"Nah, yeah I need this like early. Wussup Tasha." I said also speaking to the other dresser.

"Hey girl." She replied glancing up from her clients hair just quick enough to make eye contact.

"Shay, wash her up real quick for me!" Karen said to her wash girl.

"OK, come on back." She said as she stood up and headed to the sinks. I followed her and took a seat

"Lean back for me." She said after wrapping the towel around my neck.

I leaned back and got comfortable as I envisioned the very gown in my closet that I wanted to wear. I had only wore I once about a year ago to a banquet I attended with Jonathan, my boyfriend at the time. He played football for the minor leagues, and they had swanky award banquets. You'd think they were the pros the way the owners pulled out all the stops for them during special occasions.

Jonathan and I had been together since junior year in high school, and remained together for five years, up until he was drafted to play overseas six months ago. I haven't seen or heard from him since.

"Damn, I can't wear that dress." I said to myself.

"Huh?" Shay asked.

"Oh nah, I was talking' to myself, my bad." I replied re-entering reality.

"Oh, so what you getting' done today?" She asked as she continued to wash my hair.

"Probably just some curls, I don't really know. I usually just let Karen do what she do, she a beast when it comes to stylin' hair." I said.

"True, I'm learning a lot from her. I was pressed to be in her class at the hair academy." Shay admitted.

"Oh yeah, you pay attention to her, you going' be a monsta too." I replied just as she turned the water off.

"That's the plan." She said wrapping the towel around my head. I went into my purse and pulled out ten dollars and passed it to her.

"Thanks boo." She said slipping it into her pocket.

"No problem." I said then I stood up and walked back out to Karen.

"Aright, i'ma' sit you up under the dryer, curl her up, then we going' make it do what it do, aright." Karen said walking over to me.

"Bet." I replied following her over to the dryer.

"Lemme' know if it's too hot." She said after sitting the dryer hood over my head and turning it on.

"Nah that's good right there." I said.

"Cool, I be back." She said walking away.

I took my phone out and got on facebook. As usual nobody was talking about shit so I threw up a status saying 'Tonight, I'm going' Lady on that ass!' Then I peeked in on a sex group that I'm in. More pictures of dicks and titties, and the thirsty asses talking about what they would do if they could.

"Boring." I said as I logged out. Then I logged in under my assumed name. When I got in, I immediately went to his wife's page. Her latest status read:

'*Hubby hanging out with his Show Off Boys tonight, so I need a ladies night, ladies what's up, we can show off too!'*

Marcus commented saying: '*But I'll be thinking about you the whole time bae'*

"Yeah, not if I have anything to do with it, nigga not on my watch!" I said to myself with a chuckle. I spent the rest of my time under the dryer looking at their pictures.

Once my hair was done and I was looking fly I paid and tipped Karen, then I headed to a boutique out Northwest and paid $250 for a gown and $70 for some heels. Then I took all back streets and made it back to my apartment by seven.

"Damn girl, look at you!" Salisha said as I walked into the apartment. She and Anthony were lying on the couch up under a blanket.

"You like?" I asked giving a playful spin.

"Hell yeah, your hair is like that. Who did it, Karen?" She asked.

"Who else?" I asked as I headed towards my room.

"I swear I gotta get her to do my hair! Hold up, you got a new dress too, where you going'?" She yelled after me.

"Out, don't wait up!" I said before closing my door.

By the time eight o'clock hit all I had to do was slip into my heels and put on my earrings. I gave myself a once over in the full length mirror, twirling around to check every angle.

"Damn, i'ma' boss bitch" I said to myself just as I heard a knock on my bedroom door.

"yeah?" I asked.

"Girl, Marcus is in the living room looking like he fell off the cover of GQ. What the fuck, you look like you fell off his arm. Where y'all going, to see the President, damn?" Salisha said speaking in a hushed tone.

"Its some big opening." I said walking towards the door.

"And he taking' *you*, and not his *wife*?" She asked. I cut my eyes at her then walked out of the room.

"yeah, they got all the talent, they just ain't doing' shit wit it." I heard Marcus say to Anthony as Salisha and I walked into the living room.

"Aright man, I'll look you up on that jont tonight." Anthony said.

46

"Bet that... Got damn shawty, that's what the fuck I'm talking bout." Marcus said when he noticed me. He took my hand and gave me a spin.

"You said badd." I replied giggling as I reveled in his attention.

"yeah, but you super badd. I see me fuckin some niggas up tonight IN my Armani." He said.

"Nah, you know where my eyes will be." I said handing him my coat.

"Oh hold up, I got you something' to complete you." He said going into his pocket. He pulled out two jewelry boxes. He opened the first one to reveal a diamond necklace.

"DAMN!" Anthony and Salisha both exclaimed.

Marcus chuckled as he put it around my neck and fastened it.

Then he opened the other box to reveal a matching diamond tennis bracelet, which he fastened around my wrist.

"Now you're complete." He said looking me up and down. I walked over to look into the mirror and fell in love with the way the jewelry accentuated the outfit.

"Marcus they are so beautiful!" I said turning around to face him. He smiled and walked over to me with my coat to place over my shoulders.

"You folks have a good evening." He said as we walked towards the door.

"You too!" Salisha said.

"Be easy." Anthony added.

We stepped out into the hallway at the same time as Steve. He and I shared a knowing look before he spoke.

"Sup dog." He said looking at Marcus.

"Sup." Marcus replied. Then Steve looked back at me.

"Have fun." He said and jogged down the steps.

When Marcus and I stepped outside I saw his Bentley parked in front of the building with the flashers on.

"The Bentley tonight huh?" I asked with a smile.

"Oh a nigga plans to show off tonight. I got my show off girl, looking' show off, and I know I'm showin' off, so I gotta have my show off car." He said as he opened the door for me. On my seat was a bouquet of long stem white roses.

"Oh my gawd, they are so beautiful" I exclaimed as I took them into my arms.

"Yeah, this is a red carpet kinda night, pulling' out all the stops. Top shelf all night." He said helping me into the car. Then he walked around and got in on his side.

"Aright, so check this out, I know I don't gotta teach you etiquette, you know how to leave the hood in the hood right." He said after he got in the car.

"Of course." I replied.

"Cool, 'cause this ain't the place for the slang, the cussing' or drama. This place is upscale, and most of the people in here are going to know each other. You may even know some folks up in here, but the moment you walk through them doors whatever you know about the person is null and void. Everybody is friends on the inside, you dig?" He asked.

"So if a chick I got beef with is in there she can't come for me and I can't go at her." I said

"Right, but y'all would take it a step forward, y'all would even be cordial. The beef would still be in y'all, and everybody that know y'all would know it, but in there, its non existent. And that's not just for beef, that's for anything. In there, it is what it is." He explained.

"And everybody in there knows that?" I asked.

"And is it wit it." He said as he started up his car.

48

**"OK" I said fastening my seat-belt.**

**We rode out to Montgomery county listening to chill, relaxing music. I always felt best when I was with him. I always tried to savor our moments together in an attempt to make them stretch. I knew that he cared about me but I wasn't stupid. I knew that we couldn't go on like this for ever, I just wanted to enjoy it while it last.**

*****

## Chapter 5

### Angel

About forty-five minutes later we pulled up to a restaurant that had a layout that could've doubled as a movie premier. It had valet parking, red carpet with the velvet rope, and big lights swerving the sky above to let people know it was there.

"WOW!" I said as we pulled up to the red carpet.

"Mr. Jones, your table is all ready for you." Said a guy who opened the door for me.

"Thanks boss, I appreciate you man." Marcus said as he slapped hands with the man. The man peeked at what Marcus gave him.

"Thank you, you're very generous sir." The man said as he stuffed it into his pocket.

"Nah man, you really deserve a lot more." Marcus said with a pat to the man's shoulder. Then he stuck his arm out for me to take.

We walked down the red carpet and into the restaurant where we were greeted by a man so huge he looked like a Sumo Wrestler.

"Zeus, aw man, where they find you at?" Marcus asked sounding excited to see him as they embraced.

"I'm always around man, you the one that got ghost an' shit." Zeus spoke with a voice that sounded as though it came from a place deep within his belly.

"No doubt, no doubt, so who in here so far?" Marcus asked as he took my hand.

"Oh the Big boys here, the fellas are here, and the Lifestyles and hustlers." He said pointing towards the middle of the restaurant.

"Bet, aright man, we gotta get up some time. My number the same, hit me up." Marcus

50

said as they slapped hands.

"No doubt homie." Zeus replied.

"Mr. Jones, right this way please." Said a man dressed as a waiter who had been waiting off to the side for the conversation to end.

Marcus gestured for me to walk out in front of him, then he slipped his arm around my waist as we followed the waiter through the gorgeous restaurant.

### Deytwon

"No this muthafucka didn't." I thought to myself as I sat in my office watching everyone below. I had been sitting in my plush lounge chair gazing out through the window that gave a bird's eye view of the goings on in and outside of my restaurant.

When I saw the Bentley pull up to the velvet rope I knew that it could only be Marcus. Not many could afford the Bentley Hunaudieres Concept.

I watched him step out and swivel around like a star showing out for the cameras. I expected him to have a Princess on his arm, as the boy never been or went for the mediocre.

I waited for the valet to open the passenger side door to reveal what I thought would be a Moroccan Princess, instead it was Angel, my future Queen.

My glass dropped from my hands as my mouth fell agape. The pieces were coming together perfectly. Now I understood why he didn't want us to approach her that day at the library. This nigga planned to fuck her himself, but why would he do that knowing that she was the Heiress? What was his angle here? I thought to myself as a rage began to boil inside me. A rage that I haven't felt in years, and never towards him. My nigga, my brother. My co heir to all the riches of this world. I had to find my chill and quick, I was ready to jump through this glass like Eazy E and fuck his ass up.

"Master, I'm sorry to disturb you, but Master Jones has arrived." Came the meek voice of my butler. He was always very careful to act very peasant like in my presence. I hated that shit, but he explained that it's his culture, and it bother him none.

"Thank you Pedro. Will you do me a favor." I said turning my attention back towards Marcus as he and Angel made their way into the restaurant.

52

"Of course Master. How may I service you?" He asked.

"Have someone clean this up for me, and please have Michaels send the best bottle of champagne to Mr. Jones and his date, compliments of me." I said.

"Yes sir of course, sir. Right away, sir." Pedro said before walking away.

Seconds later Garsceon my cleaning attendant came in and cleaned the stain from the carpet, while Thomas my bartender handed me another drink. I tipped them each before asking to be left alone.

"Well played my friend, well played." I said raising my glass in the air towards Marcus as I watched him and Angel take their seats.

To my knowledge he had never crossed me before, but from this lesson he will learn to never cross me again.

## Angel

The layout in the restaurant was so fabulous with the sparkling crystal chandeliers, statues and art work strategically placed about. The tables were dressed with satin table clothes, topped with candles and a vase filled with fresh flowers. The tables were situated around a water fountain that shot water up towards a glass ceiling that revealed the sky.

"Wow." I said as I looked around.

"yeah, I know right." Marcus said nodding his head in agreement.

"How does this table suit you sir?" The waiter asked stopping at a table that sort of sat on a platform above the rest. It was next to a picture window which overlooked a lake.

"Perfectly." Marcus said smiling in approval.

"Very good sir. Should I check your coats sir?" The waiter asked as Marcus pulled my coat from my shoulders.

"Yes sir I'd appreciate that." Marcus said speaking properly. He took off his coat and handed it to the waiter.

"Thank you sir, may you have an enchanting evening." The waiter said.

Thanks boss, you as well." Marcus said as he shook the waiters hand. I watched as the waiter peaked at what Marcus gave him, noting that he was surprised.

"Thank you sir, you are most generous." The waiter say cheerfully.

"I appreciate your service." Marcus said as he pulled my chair out for me.

"My nigga, we were wondering when you were gonna fall in." Said a guy as he walked over to Marcus.

"How everybody going see me, if I don't interrupt the show, ya dig?" Marcus replied as they did a hug handshake.

"Nigga always showin off, so what you think? Rich ass always go too far!" The guy said looking around the restaurant.

"We big boys, we supposed to, what the fuck." Marcus said.

"No muthafuckin doubt. Aye, yall go head get comfortable, drink up, eat up, we going' take pics in a lil bit." The guy said.

"Who, us and them?" Marcus asked confused.

"The fuck nigga, that's that Russian roulette shit right there. Niggas 'a make posters outta evidence like that, have all of us all the way fucked up. Nah, get your couple on, on ya own time." The guy said

"No bullshit. Aright nigga, i'ma' mellow in and I'll get up with y'all." Marcus said.

"Aright man." The guy said as they slapped hands.

"So I thought you said no slang and no cussing." I said after Marcus sat down.

"I said that for *you*. I ain't come here *not* to have a lady on my arm." He replied casually.

"Oh, I'm all lady, all day." I sassed.

"Good, then play your part. You are shining like a star tonight though." He said.

"That's what I am." I blushed.

"Bet that, there's an after party up at the Gay-lord. I got a suite for after, you staying' with me?" He asked as he leaned towards me and rubbed my thigh under the table.

"Of course, but why didn't you tell me, I would've packed an over night bag." I replied ready to jump on him.

"That's why. Money don't walk into the Gay-lord in a suit and walk out in a t-shirt. I got you when we leave here." He said as he sat back.

"But what's open this time of night?" I asked.

"Angel, I'm about to introduce you to a little bit of my world. I'm not just some anything ass nigga out here ripping up the streets. All I need you to do is chill out, don't question what I tell you. If I say it, it either is, or will be. You got it?" He asked.

I nodded my head confused.

"Should I be worried?" I asked feeling a little overwhelmed that Marcus wasn't all the way who I thought he was.

"You plan to cross me?" He asked.

"Of course not." I answered.

"Then of course not." He replied with a shrug as he sat back in his seat.

"Aw shit, I see we got the big boys in the muthafuckin' house!" A guy said as he walked over to Marcus.

"My nigga." Marcus said as he stood to hug the guy.

"My nigga for real, what's been up? Ain't seen yo ass in a tight grip!" The guy said.

"Chilling, doing what I do, what about you, what happened with that?" Marcus asked.

I rolled my eyes and just scanned the room. I had become bored with these conversations that left me feeling neglected.

None of the people he spoke with acknowledged me, other than giving a look that said *'damn'* but even that was quick. While I did find it odd that Marcus didn't introduce me to anyone, I didn't want to ruin the night by making a fuss over it. I was just happy to be with him, and now that I knew I was spending the night with him I was all the way boosted.

The place was packed out. Everyone, men and women were dressed in some type of classy attire. I noticed that the women were all seated looking fabulous, but looked bored while the men

56

stood in groups talking and laughing it up.

A few moments later groves of waiters came out all holding a bottle of wine and 2 glasses.

"Aright dog, I holla." I heard Marcus say before he took his seat.

"Domaine Faiveley Musigny Grand Cru, Cote de Nuits, France, sir, compliments of Mr. Richards." The waiter said presenting our bottle of wine to us over his arm.

"Excellent." Marcus replied as our glasses were sat on the table before us.

"Very good sir." The waiter said then he opened the bottle and poured the wine into our glasses.

"You have been most wonderful." Marcus said shaking the waiters hand.

"My pleasure Sir." The waiter replied with a smile.

"Here's to The Big Boys, The Fellas, The Life Styles and The Hustlers, on behalf of Mr. Richards. Welcome to the grand opening of Sides. Cheers to the good life." A man standing on stage said.

"Cheers." sang the crowd.

"What were all those groups he named?" I asked wondering if they were gangs.

"Never talk before you sip after a toast." Marcus said after putting his glass back down. I looked at him confused before taking a sip of the wine.

"Damn that's good." I said never have tasted wine that I liked.

"It should be, it's over two thousand dollars." He replied.

"You just bought a bottle of wine that cost..." I started but was cut off by Marcus putting a finger up.

"One, he just said it was compliments of the host, two, does money excite you? Let me know that shit now." He said sounding annoyed. I sat back in my seat feeling a little embarrassed.

"No, I was just shocked." I replied.

"Well i'ma' need you to handle your shock better, because this is the tip of the iceberg, you ain't seen shit yet, and I need to know that you can handle it before I bring you in." He said.

"I'm good." I replied. Marcus nodded his head at me before taking another sip.

"Gentlemen and ladies, 'Good Hope'." Said another man who took the stage. Seconds later the curtains opened to reveal a live band, with a woman in front holding a Mic.

"Do you dance?" Marcus asked as they began to play.

"I haven't danced to a slow song in a long time." I replied thinking about Jonathan and I at the prom.

"Then you're about due." Marcus said as he took my hand and lead me to the dance floor with the other couples.

He put my arms around his neck, and took my waist and pulled me close before he started to move.

"Just look into my eyes, and follow my lead." He said.

We danced through three songs before someone came to whisper in his ear.

"Bet." He replied to the man who then walked away.

"Angel, I'm about to go handle some business. Go back to the table, order something to eat, anything you want, and I'll be back." He said as he snapped his finger for a waiter to come over.

"But I don't know what to order, I never saw the menu." I replied.

"There are no menus, order whatever you feel like eating. Hey boss, will you escort her back to the table for me." Marcus said to me then to the waiter.

58

"Gladly sir." The waiter replied.

"I really appreciate it." Marcus said as he shook the waiters hand.

"But I need to use the restroom." I whispered to Marcus.

"Cool, escort her to the restroom, then back to the table." Marcus said shaking the waiters hand again. Then he looked at me, and leaned in to kiss me behind the ear.

"You are looking so fuckin gorgeous tonight." He whispered to me before stepping off. I blushed all over myself.

"This way madam." The waiter said holding his arm out.

Once I finished in the restroom I stepped out to see the waiter standing across the way waiting on me.

"Shall we madam?" He asked slightly bent forward as though he were bowing.

"No, actually, I will escort her, you may go." I heard a familiar voice say as the person shook hands with the waiter.

"Yes sir Mr. Richards." The waiter said before walking away.

"What are you doing here?" I asked shocked when Deytwon, the guy who tried to holla at me a couple days ago turned around to face me.

"Shouldn't the owner be at his grand opening. That would be some tacky shit if I weren't, don't you think?" He asked with a smile.

"So this is all you?" I asked.

"yeah, this is what I call my hobby." He replied.

"This is some hobby, my hobby is poetry, by the way." I said.

"That's what's up, so, I see your Marcus's arm candy, huh?" He asked.

"How do you know that I'm not his wife?" I asked with my hand on my hip.

"For three reasons, one, I know Marcus, and his wife. Two, if you were his wife, you damn sure wouldn't be working at Shopper. And three, he wouldn't have brought you here." He said

"Why not?" I asked very curious as it was strange that he'd bring me to something like this and not his wife.

"Because I made *this* restaurant specifically for the ballers to bring their side chicks, hence the name 'Sides'." He explained.

My heart dropped all the way down into my shoes. Every time I thought I was moving up in importance in Marcus' life I was knocked all the way back down to the bottom.

I had no reply, I simply shook my head.

"You good?" He asked.

"No, I'm not. Why are you telling me this anyway?" I asked lashing out at him.

"You didn't know you were a *Side chick*?" He asked looking confused.

"I knew, of course I know that, I just.." I started but stopped, I had nothing to say, what could I say when I was just as wrong as Marcus.

"You just want to be more." Deytwon said sounding as though he understood.

"Yeah." I replied softly, shaking my head.

"Then be more." He replied.

"But, I love him." I admitted.

"So then this is worth it to you, and cool for the rest of your life, because he will never leave her." He said.

I looked down and shook my head once again thinking '*Fuck my life!*'

"You still got my card?" He asked.

"Yeah." I replied.

"Use it when you've had enough." He said.

"Why, so that I can become *your* side chick?" I asked with an attitude.

"I'm not married, and I don't do side chicks. I need one woman that I can continue my empire with. Like I told you, I don't need a game player, only a game changer" He said.

"Then why sponsor this place that encourages something you don't believe in?" I asked.

"Because I believe in making money, I'm capitalizing on what these niggas do for fun." He explained.

"But a place like this, you're spending a lot of money." I said looking around.

"I do, because I'm not a half ass nigga. If I'ma' do it, I'm going to the ends of the earth with it. But believe me, they spend more on living the hush life. But anyway, if you want to have something to say about any of this, you'll use the number I gave you." He said.

"Why me?" I asked wondering why he wanted me.

"That's what I'm trying to find out." He replied.

"My man Deytwon. What's good nigga, digging' the shit out of the place." Marcus said as he walked up and put his arm around me.

"My man, I knew you would. How you like that wine I sent you?" Deytwon asked with a chuckle.

"Coming' from you man, it's what I expect, boss shit." Marcus said.

"From a boss to a boss." Deytwon replied.

"No doubt, aright man, I'm 'bout to go get something to eat before we take these pics, I holla."Marcus said before shaking hands with him.

"Bet that." Deytwon replied before Marcus and I walked away.

"Whateva that nigga said to you, keep in mind that my wife used to be his girl. He loved her and ain't been with nobody since. So if he was throwing' salt, that's the source." Marcus mumbled in my ear as we approached the table.

"He wasn't throwing salt." I said. Marcus just looked at me in disbelief while snapping for the waiter.

*****

## Chapter 6

### Angel

Later that night we reconvened at a club on the top floor of the Gay-lord. The room was semi dark with party lights swirling and flashing. There were women in cages dancing in all four corners of the room, and half naked women walking about as though their breast hanging out for all to see was normal, and natural. There were groups of men standing around talking, and other groups shot pool, played cards, domino's and dice.

"Wow, are these the same people from the restaurant?" I asked confused as we walked through the place.

"Some of them are, some are just guests. If you stick around long enough, you'll be able to tell the difference." He said as we walked by a couch where two men were having sex with one woman.

"Damn, this is a hotel, why don't they just get a room?" I asked as I slipped my arm around Marcus's arm for added comfort.

"You think that's bad, wait till we get towards the back. In here, anything goes, just as long as its not done against a big boy or his guest." He said with a chuckle as he walked on.

"Whats a big boy" I asked growing very curious as I've been hearing the phrase all night.

"I am a big boy." He said showing me a ring on his pinky finger. It was a platinum ring with the letters 'BB' underneath three diamonds .

"So what is that, some kind of fraternity?" I asked.

"In a lot of ways, yes." He replied.

"My man, glad you could make it." Said a guy who slapped hands with Marcus.

"How often do the big boys get together? Of course I made it." Marcus replied as a man in a suit slid his coat from his arms.

"No doubt. So come on back, the boys and the fellas are having an emergency meeting. Since Sean's been released, we gotta make sure we fuck that case into oblivion, can't have our future big boy doing life." The guy said.

"If I loved my wife as much as he loves his youngin', I would've done the same thing. But as it stands, I would've just sent the goons after his bitchass." Marcus said as he was handed a drink.

"He said he could feel the fear in her when she saw the nigga, while they were at the mall that day. It was too much, cuz did what he had to do." The guy said.

"No doubt. So look, you got a ribbon for me? Marcus said glancing from me back to the guy.

"Fa' sho'." The guy said as he pulled a silver ribbon from his pocket.

"Thanks man, see you back there." Marcus said before turning his attention to me.

"Look, I need you to wear this until you see me again. Don't take it off, don't fidget with it, just wear it and make sure its always visible." Marcus said as he snapped it around my neck.

"What's this for?" I asked.

"So niggas wont fuck wit'chu while I'm gone. You'll be taken care of as long as you have that on tonight." He explained.

"But, I don't understand, where are you going?" I asked feeling apprehensive about being in this crazy atmosphere alone.

"I have a meeting to go to. Chill out, you going' be good, long as you have that on." He said.

64

"So you want me to stay out here with *THEM*?!" I asked. The room looked like a seedy back alley. I couldn't believe he was leaving me in the midst of imminent danger.

"Listen, have I ever let anything happen to you while you were with me?" He asked

"No, but I'm not about to be with you now." I said.

"As long as you have this around your neck, you are with me, this is my protection for you. As long as you don't take it off, you'll be good." He said.

"What happens if I take it off?" I asked

"Everything. That girl out there, getting fucked by them two dudes, she don't want that shit. They're raping her." He said said casually.

"What, why isn't anyone stopping it?!" I gasped as the harsh reality of his world began to bite.

"That's the price you pay. No one is forced to come here, but they do, to get at us. The sad thing is, she may not even get noticed by a big boy or even a fella. But to her... this shit is worth it." He said shaking his head.

I shook my head as my mind tried to process the shit he just told me. Why would he bring me here, is this a warning for what could happen if I did cross him?

"You are good, just don't forget yourself out there. A few of them chicks in the cages, a few of them chicks doing' chalk lines, a few of them chicks getting taken, use to be side chicks that thought they could handle their liquor, or thought they could handle the chalk, or got mad at their big boy and took the ribbon off. Once you do that, you'll become just another face in that crowd, and whatever happens to you, happens." He said.

My stomach began to turn, I was starting to feel as though I had wandered into a dimension of hell. What the fuck was this nigga really into, and what did I let him stroke me into?

"You good shawty?" He asked with a chuckle.

"Yeah, just hurry please, I want to get out of here." I said.

"Bet that." He replied before turning to walk away.

"Madam, would you like to have a seat?" The man who took Marcus's coat asked me.

"Yes, please." I said. I followed him back through the room. I forced my eyes to look up in order to avoid seeing everything that was going on. Problem was I couldn't avoid hearing the cries and the screams, or the wicked sounding laughter, and guys demanding that someone pays up.

The mere fact that Marcus brought me here only further served to show me that he didn't care nearly as much about me as I do him. This place was horrible, and I couldn't stand it. I was far from a saint, but how could I feel comfortable sitting back allowing another to be in pain, when they did nothing wrong to me.

### Marcus

"I'm saying' joe, I'm hood man, my girl hood. What we gonna do in another country?" Sean said with a chuckle after gulping down his beer. Sean was my nigga, one of the realest still on the streets.

The Big Boys just helped him beat a murder charge on the strength that he was to be our newest inductee. Sean didn't come from money the way most of us did. He came straight off the block. He made money and he saved money, now he was ready to be a contender in the Big Boys ranks. He wasn't high in, because his money didn't stretch as long as others, especially the born heirs, but he had the heart of a leader which is why we took to him the way we did.

After the restaurant opening we decided to have an inductee ceremony for him over at the Gay-lord I brought Angel along because I needed the sex. Of all the side ass I had, no bitch could fuck and suck me like her, and since the wife was on, I wasn't about to go there.

"Look man, you're a Big Boy now, just do what you do. But I'm telling you, the world is bigger than DC, you just gotta go Christopher Columbus and find that shit out for yourself." I said before taking a sip of my drink..

## Angel

"So you're here." I heard Deytwon's voice ask as the man in the suit and I were making our way across the room. I turned around to see him standing in the middle of the room.

"Yes, but I don't know why." I said very upset.

"Because, you're not the wife." He answered.

"Are you being paid to remind me of that, or what?" I asked annoyed.

"Are you being paid to forget?" He asked back.

"What do you want from me?" I asked ready to run out of this place.

"I want you." He answered.

"You don't even know me, and aren't you and Marcus friends?" I asked.

"We are associates." He said.

"What the hell does that mean?" I asked more angry at being in the place than I was at Deytwon's advances.

"We are not friends." He said.

"I can't deal with this right now, I just want to get the hell out of here! This place is too much!" I said looking around.

"Then go." Deytwon said as though it only made sense.

"I cant leave, I came with him." I said.

"Did you tell him that you didn't want to be here?" He asked.

"Yes." I replied.

"But you are still here." He said.

"He has a meeting, he cant just go." I explained.

"Not even for you? Knowing that this place is fuckin with you?" Deytwon asked.

"Deytwon stop it. You and I both know that he doesn't love me." I said as tears came to my eyes.

"Do *you*, love you?" He asked.

"What, of course I love myself." I replied.

"That remains to be seen." He replied.

"You get a kick out of judging me, don't you?" I asked as I wiped my eyes.

"About as much of a kick as you get out of wiping the same tears. Take her to the V.I.P" He said as he put something in the guy in the suits hand.

"Yes sir." The guy in the suit said.

"This isn't fun for me." I said.

"Neither is watching you go through it, but what can we do but allow nature to take its course." He asked before nodding his head at the guy in the suit and turning to leave.

The guy in the suit lead me to the V.I.P section where there were more lights, a long buffet of delicious foods, soft music and a helluva lot less back alley shit.

### Marcus

"I feel you, I'll see what's up wit my shawty and go from there. She been through a lot. She could use a lil vaycay." Sean continued.

"That's what I'm talking about, man." I said before glancing out of the two way window of the conference room to see Angel talking with Deytwon, *again.*"

"Oh yeah?" I said more to myself.

"What's good?" Sean asked looking out in the same direction trying to see what I was talking about.

"Nah, it's cool. So look, if you need anything don't hesitate, you hear me?" I said redirecting the conversation back to Sean.

"No doubt. I appreciate that." Sean replied as we slapped hands.

"Fuck it's so quiet in this bitch, let's party!" I shouted as the elite group of strippers entered the conference room.

I took up my drink and glanced back towards Angel and Deytwon to see her run her hand across her cheek. Seconds later my man Deytwon slipped something to the waiter, and then Angel and the waiter stepped off.

I guess that nigga was more into her than I thought. It ain't enough to him to know that I'm fuckin her. Nah, I gotta go harder. Time to turn the shit up a lil more. I had a spot in Georgetown that was unused, guess it's about to finally get an occupant.

If Deytwon keeps making me turn up the heat, i'ma' fuck around and not just make sure Angel ain't no good for him, she ain't gonna be no good for nobody. If he really love her, he'd best leave her alone. I thought to myself

**"Mmhmm." I said just before throwing back my drink..**

**\*\*\*\***

**<> Deytwon <>**

**Seeing Angel on Marcus' arm really threw me for a loop. I wasn't ready for that unexpected shit at all. She seemed really taken by him too, which posed a big problem for me, because now my mission became operation recovery. No doubt he was sexing' her, which also fucked me up, but I was starting to understand why, and it was for that very reason that I knew he planned to dog her something serious. Nevertheless, my plan to wife her didn't change, I still wanted her because I still got the urge that she was my missing piece when I was around her.**

**She seemed cool, just very lost. Like she was searching for something undefinable, and was settling for whatever it was that Marcus was giving her. Off conversation with her alone, it wasn't hard to see that getting her was easy, and by Marcus being a master manipulator, I'm sure he was getting good use out of her. But whatever he was destroying inside her, I was preparing myself to restore.**

**Its sad how he allowed himself to be consumed with the love of power to the point where he had no limits obtaining it. Its even sadder when the very thing you love becomes your undoing.**

**Never start a war that you only think you can win. Underestimating your opponent underestimates your ability to survive, especially with an opponent like myself.**

## Chapter 7

### Angel

Three hours later, Marcus' meeting finally ended, so he came to find me and took me down to the hotel suite. He was very quiet during the elevator ride and walk to the room. His silence was an indication that something was on his mind, but I didn't want to inquire I just wanted to get out of these clothes and into a shower. I knew that whatever he'd been thinking would come out anyway. He never had a problem speaking his mind.

When we got to the suite he opened the door for me and flicked on the lights. I walked down a little hall which led to a living room like area, equipped with a couch, coffee table, lounge chairs, and a 42 inch TV that was mounted to the wall.

Behind the living room space was a sort of dinning area space, equipped with a large dining room table, a buffet table and painting on the walls. It even had a balcony that over looked the atrium.

Marcus walked back to the bedroom while I peered over the balcony/ I looked around the room in complete awe, it was set up like a huge one bedroom apartment.

"You good?" I asked after finally meeting him in the room. He had been typing something into his phone.

"I'm great." He replied looking up from his phone.

"OK, well, I'm going to get into the shower." I said as I walked towards the bathroom.

"Yeah, do that." He replied. I looked back at him to see that he had returned his attention to his phone.

Once I was finished in the shower, I used some of the hotel lotion for women, which smelled like heaven, then I wrapped a towel around myself and went back into the bedroom. Through the doors I saw Marcus was was sitting on the back of the couch smoking a jay,

"Marcus, you sure you good?" I asked standing in the doorway between the bedroom and the dinning room.

He stood up and walked over to a glass of liquor he apparently poured himself while I was in the shower, and dropped the jay inside. Then he walked over to me, undid my towel and let it drop to the floor.

"I see you're ready." I said smiling as he lift me up and pulled my legs around his waist.

He carried me over to the bed where he dropped me, then he took off his clothes and reached for a condom.

"I'ma' do something different tonight." He said as he worked the condom on.

"Oh yeah, whats that?" I asked smiling and ready, at least I thought I was until he flipped me over.

Suddenly I felt him guiding his dick into my ass with one hand and held me down by the back of my neck with the other.

"Marcus, what the fuck, you ain't using' nothing'?!" I yelled. He didn't reply as he rammed his dick inside my ass as far as it could go. I screamed from the shot of pain that tore up my rectum.

He started long stroking it, forcibly pushing and pulling into my virgin ass like I was a pro at taking anal. All the while he held me down by the back of my neck.

"Marcus, please!" I cried as he kept driving his dick in and out.

"Ready to talk?" He asked

"About what, oww, gotdamn!" I shouted.

"Why the fuck every time I leave you alone, you wind up talking' to Deytwon. The fuck is going' on with that bullshit?!" He asked never losing his rhythm,

"Nothing, nothing I swear! I met him a few days ago while I was at work! I didn't even know who he was, and I never gave him my number, I told him I wasn't interested! He was just surprised to see me, please Marcus, stop!" I cried.

"I told you, me and that nigga not cool, so why the fuck don't you carry him like you would do any other nigga? Why you be talking' to him for so long? What the fuck yall got to say to each other?"! He asked.

"Nothing! He just asked me if I was happy being a side chick. I told him I just wanted to be with you, and I didn't care!" I cried.

"So what he have to say about that?" Marcus asked as he slowed down the stroke.

"Just that I should learn to love myself." I replied now crying as those words began to ring so true in my ears right now.

Marcus pulled his dick all the way out and rolled me over onto my back.

"I'm counting on you, to never fuckin lie to me, do you understand me. I am not the nigga you want to lie to, I am vile and I am unforgiving." He said leaning over top of me looking me dead in my eyes.

I nodded my head in fear as the tears continued to roll down my face. He leaned in to kiss my neck, and continued to kiss down my body until he was between my legs eating me out.

The next morning I woke up to the smell of sweet Belgium waffles and coffee. I eased out of bed and painfully made my way to the bathroom. Afterwords I went out to join Marcus at the breakfast table.

"I ain't know what you eat, so I just ordered a lil bit of everything, eat up." He said

74

sounding like the old Marcus I knew before being introduced to his way of life.

There was a small buffet of breakfast foods, bacon, sausage, grits, pancakes, waffles, biscuits, hash browns, eggs, toast, muffins, oatmeal, fruits, everything a person could want to eat.

"Smells good." I said as I grabbed a plate and walked over to the buffet.

"So, after breakfast I got some clothes coming in for you to check out. Pick out a couple outfits and some shoes and accessories that you like. Told you, gotta leave here classy." He said before sipping his orange juice.

"OK" I replied as I continued getting my food.

After breakfast I went to take a shower, when I came back out there was a robe and a pair of panties and bra laying across the bed for me.

I put on the panties and bra, then I grabbed the robe before leaving out of the room.

"yeah, this is a good selection, yeah, this'll work." I heard Marcus say as I walked into the living room area. He had been out there talking with a woman as they looked through a rack of clothing and accessories.

"These are the clothes?" I asked to get his attention, and to block as I noticed Ms Thing seemed to be flirting with him.

"Aw, yeah, this is Trisha, she's a stylist, she be having' all the fly shit. Trish, this is Angel, your lump of clay." Marcus said introducing us.

"Nice to meet you. You got a nice shape, I got a lot here that will compliment the shit out of you." Trisha said.

"That's what I'm talking' 'bout. Aright ladies, get it. I'll be back." Marcus said as he headed for the door. I looked over at him wanting to ask where he was going, but didn't want to get carried in front of this woman.

Sidechick Blues The Plot by Nikida Bellezza

"OK, so if you'll just come over here and have a look, we can get started. Just to let you know, he likes everything, so really whatever you pick out will work for him." She said.

"Aright." I replied walking over to the clothes rack.

There were all styles of clothes from ball gowns, to business suits, to chilling' with money outfits. They all looked nice, but none of them were me. I was a chilling' in my stretch pants and cute shirt with boots type chick. For me to wear the things I saw on this rack, I'd have to be going some place really nice.

"Whats wrong?" Trisha asked as she watched me push through the clothing.

"I mean, this stuff is nice, but its not me. Where the fuck am I going that I need to wear a shirt like this, I mean, its cute, but I don't do shit that requires this outfit." I said holding up an off the shoulder shirt

"Not yet, but you will, trust me, if he got me here, he got plans for you." Trisha said as she pulled out a pair of pants and some thigh high boots that complimented the shirt well.

"What you know about it?" I asked confused.

"I'm just saying', I don't work for a company. I'm contracted through the Big Boys. I make enough money working with them, that I don't need no more clients. And they only call me when they got big plans for a chick." She explained as she began to sift through more clothing.

"Big plans like what? And what the hell are the Big Boys?" I asked intrigued.

"Look, all I can tell you is, stay grounded, play your cards right and never go left. The Big Boys are a group of black men who are worth a certain amount of money. Its like a Secret Society, only they're not really a secret, they're well known amongst the elite, they're very powerful, and that's all I know." She said.

"So then who are the fella's and the rest of them?" I asked

"The fellas got money, but they don't have as much as the Big Boys, they often partner with the Big Boys when they want to get things done, they're not a bad team either, they just don't have as much power. Now, the lifestyles live comfortably, but their money don't stretch as long as the fellas, and damn sure not as much as the Big Boys. The hustlers are just that, they hustle, they lock the streets, they can make power moves, but all of their OK's have to come from the Big Boys. They got money, but they mostly attract anything type females. Them the ones the hood rats be laid up with." She explained volunteering info that I didn't ask for.

"Wow." I was in awe, never did I suspect any of this when I met Marcus. He just seemed like a cool guy to be with who gave me bomb ass sex. Now to know that he was this powerful nigga living by his own rules, it gave me a very strange feeling inside. I didn't know whether to run, or to stay and see where this road would take me. Although by judging from the way he went crazy on me last night, I knew shit could get way worse, just because of the amount of power he had.

"Look, don't let me scare you away, this is the good life. Just, don't drown in the shit. Be good to him, stay loyal, and try to build on this fertile ass land. He toss you a couple dollars, toss that shit in the bank and let it grow, then start a business or something." She said.

"How did you get involved in all this?" I asked.

"Long story, not even worth tellin', come on lets get you something to wear." She said going back through the clothing.

*'Oh yeah bitch, now I really wanna know.'* I thought to myself as I felt that she knew more than she was letting on. The way she gave up information, I knew that it wouldn't be hard to find out what I wanted to know, but for now I would just play her close and keep friendly with her informant ass.

## Chapter 8

### Angel

Two weeks after the Gay-lord event, I was standing at a curb side in Georgetown, DC, watching as moving men carried my things from several vans into my new condo. Marcus said he wanted me to have my own place, in an upscale location, so that I could get used to dealing with high society. He made me quit my job at shoppers the day after we left the hotel and has been footing all of my bills since.

"Hi, I'm Sue, are you just moving in?" Asked a very chipper tanned blond.

"Yes, Angel." I replied extending my hand to meet hers. Normally I would've laughed at her, but Marcus told me to leave the ghetto in the ghetto, so I had to square myself up in order to fit into this ritzy area.

"Awesome, I live on the 8th floor. If you ever need anything just ask. My friends and I are going clubing this weekend, think you'd be interested?" She asked bouncing as she spoke. She was very happy, she had the kind of innocent happiness a child has before the world reveals itself to them.

"Uhm, no thanks, but thank you for including me. I'm sure I'll see you around." I replied forcing an enthusiastic smile.

"Cool, well, have fun, you're going to totally love it here, I swear!" She said with a tap to my arm before running off.

"Oh my gawd." I said to myself as I followed the movers into my new place.

When I reached my apartment I saw the men taking my things out of the box and placing them into their proper location. I was very impressed with how quickly they worked and

78

Sidechick Blues The Plot by Nikida Bellezza

wondered about the tip they'd get, or knowing Marcus, probably already got.

"Hescuse me miss, these are your personal things, where you want them?" One of the guys asked as he approached me with a box marked bedroom.

"I'll take them, thank you." I said taking them out of his hands.

I walked back to the bedroom and sat the box on the floor next to a huge window that caught my eye. I gazed out at the scenery, a beautiful view of the city. I just couldn't get over having such a view, and a bay window to see it all from.

"So how you like the place?" Marcus' voice startled me into reality.

"Huh? Oh I love it. This place is like that." I said as I walked over to him.

"yeah, we gotta do something' 'bout your use of slang. This ain't the place for it, these people hear you talk slang, they going' think you're affiliated with some kinda gang or something." He said as I eased my arms around him.

"I can turn it on or off." I replied.

"yeah? Lets test that, what you think of this place?" He asked stepping out of my embrace.

"Its wonderful, simply beautiful." I replied drifting my arms into the air.

"My girl." He replied with a chuckle.

"Hescuse me Sir, we are finished, is there anything else you need?" A worker asked as he stood in the door way.

"Nah, thanks man, you guys did good. Here you go, share that with your buddies OK" Marcus said after going into his pocket and pulling out some money.

"Thank you sir, any time you need us, we be at home depot, just come look for us, we'll be ready." The guy said after receiving the wad of money.

"Alright, I'll hold you to that." Marcus replied with a pat on the mans back.

"So what's good, you trying' go get something to eat?" He asked once he turned his attention back towards me.

"I would be delighted." I replied with a curtsy.

"Too much." He said shaking his head.

"OK then, I would be delighted." I replied with my hands on my hips and a raised eyebrow.

"Aright, well, dress regular, we just going get some short shit, then I gotta jet. I got somewhere to be later." He said as he yawned and stretched.

"So hold up, I gotta spend my first night here alone?" I asked

"What's the problem?" He asked confused.

"I thought you was going stay with me." I whined

"Over night?" He asked still looking confused.

"yeah." I replied with my hands on my hips.

He shook his head as he let out a chuckle.

"Slim, how many more times we gotta have this type of conversation before you get it?" He asked.

"You know what, never mind, let me get in the shower so we can roll." I said now shaking my own head.

"Nah, fuck that, you killed my mood, I'm not even hungry now." He said as he left my room.

"What the fuck, so where you going now?" I asked following him out of the room.

"Shawty, you blowin the shit out of me right now, I'm 'bout to just dip. I got better shit to do than argue." He said.

"Yeah, you make that shit clear all the time. So what I'm supposed to do? There's no food in here." I said.

"That's right, here slim, this is a debit card. I put five thousand on here. I got your bills, this is for you. I don't want to see a rack of tennis shoes and jeans, I need you in some classy shit, like all the time. I'm loading' five G's a month on here. You need to look like money. The classier you get the more I'll load, but i'ma' start you at five." He said after going into his wallet to retrieve a platinum visa card.

"So on my first night, I'm eating dinner alone?" I asked as I took the card.

"Damn shawty, I just gave you five G's When the last time you seen five G's?" He asked indicating that I was ungrateful.

"Forever putting me in my place. OK, thank you Marcus. Enjoy the rest of your evening." I said before turning to leave.

"Tell me you tired of this shit, and we can put it to a halt now." He called behind me.

I turned around to face him, he was leaning against the wall staring down at his phone.

"Can you do me a favor?" I asked.

"Oh, I'm *not*?" He asked looking up at me.

"Young, do your asshole mic always gotta be on? I mean, do you ever turn that shit off?" I asked folding my arms.

"What's up slim." He asked with a sigh.

"Put yourself in my shoes, if someone was doing *you* the way you doing *me*, how would you feel?" I asked upset.

"First of all shawty, we two different people, shit like this will never happen to me. Second,

81

you act like I'm this cold ass nigga to you. But every since I came around, you don't want for shit,

so I'm really findin' it hard to understand your beef." He said.

"I do want for something, but its too expensive for you to front me." I sassed.

"Oh yeah, what's that?" He asked with a chuckle.

"Your time." I replied.

"What the fuck, am I a hologram right now? I'm not really here?" He asked.

"You know what I mean. I can barely squeeze a damn hour out of you, and you're ready to

go right now." I said.

"Same 'ol shit, just a different day." He sighed as he looked back down at his phone.

"What do you want with me? You just want some ready made pussy? Is that it?" I asked.

"I got that shit in my wife." He replied.

"Then what the fuck am I doing here?" I asked.

"You tell me." He said.

"I got caught up in my feelings." I replied.

"See, that's where you fucked up." He said still looking down at his phone again.

"FUCK YOU!" I shouted before going into my room. I lay on my bed and let the tears

flow. I hated that he had me the way that he did. It was bad enough he had my heart, but this

nigga also had me physically. I had no family to fall back on, the best I could do was live with

friends, and my options with that were next to none. I let the tears fall as I began to feel sorry for

myself.

A few seconds later I heard him come into my room. He got in bed with me and put his

arms around me.

"Just go, Marcus." I said wiping away my tears.

82

He turned me over to face him then he softly kissed my neck.

"You know I fuck with you slim, but you gotta know, this shit *is* what it is." He whispered to me.

"I don't have anybody else." I said.

"That's why I got your back, but you cant keep confusing this shit. I got a wife, I don't mean to be carrying you, but I cant have you confusing your position." He said.

"I know, its just hard to be alone sometimes." I said.

"I get that, trust me, baby girl, I come when I can." He said

I put my arms around him and held him close.

I knew and understood that he was not mine, that he will never be mine, I just needed these few seconds of make believe time.

"Take off your clothes." He whispered.

I stood up next to the bed and slowly took off my clothing. He pulled out a condom and put it on after taking off his clothes, then he came over to me and walked me backwards until I was against the wall.

He leaned in and kissed my neck soft and slow before trailing kisses down to my breast where he sucked and teased them until they were standing at attention. My eyes rolled as I felt him ease one then two fingers inside me.

"Damn shawty, you ready for daddy huh?" He whispered in my ear.

"Always." I whispered back as I put my arms around his waist to pull him against me to feel his dick poke at my clit.

"That's that shit I'm talking' bout right there. You want that long stroke, or you want me to beat it?" He asked.

"Both, but mostly beat it." I said.

"Bet that." He said as he lift me up on his waist. He guided himself inside me and shot it straight up inside.

"*Ohhhhhhhhh SHIT*!" I yelled from the pleasure and pain. I wasn't ready! I held onto him for dear life as he rolled and thrust his hips upward inside me until I couldn't take it anymore.

I let out a loud moan and I tightened my thighs around him.

"That's right cum for me, choke this dick." He said as he continued to pound inside me.

When I was done coming I lay limp against him. He eventually carried me over to the bed where he lay down leaving me on top.

"Ride me." he said with a slap to my ass.

I sat up and and danced on his dick, dipping, rocking, rolling and gyrating my hips while tightening my muscles until he had no choice but to give up the orgasm.

"Awwww shiiit, got dam!" He said holding on to my headboard.

Afterwords I rolled off of him and lie flat on my back and continued to enjoy the natural high.

"Shawty, your head and hip skills is why I always gotta keep you on tap. You too beastly with that shit! Got damn" He said.

All I could do was smile up at the ceiling. It was like that Wale song, I never made love, but I sure knew how to fuck the shit out of a nigga.

Marcus and I lie there on the bed for a little longer, then he ordered some fancy meal from a restaurant that delivered. We ate, talked then he rolled out.

It was always hard for me to see him go, especially when I knew he was leaving to be with another woman who happened to be his wife. I knew that I was wrong, but my addiction to him was so strong and I saw no means of escape, and to be honest, I didn't even know if I wanted to.

****

## Chapter 9

### Angel

Over the course of the next few months Marcus allegedly found hi

.36+0mself in many meetings which served to sever even more of the amount of time we had to

spend together. In the interim of shopping and being bored half to death, I had decided to use

some of the money he was giving me to sign up for school over at UDC.

Since I had such a love for poetry, I decided to take a few courses in creative writing, and

literature. I was doing pretty good too, my professors often used my work as the guidelines for

creativity and structure. I loved it, for the first time I was in the lead for something in my life.

Every now and then I'd give Salisha a call to check up on her and to let her know that I

was OK She often worried about me like a big sister. I loved having someone in my life that had

my back. She told me that she let Anthony move in to help her make the rent, but truth be told,

she made enough money to cover her rent, I think she just didn't want to live alone.

I never kept in contact with Steve, which was really fucked up because he was my nigga

like shit. But I felt it would be wrong to call another nigga on Maarcus' dime.

Basically my nights where spent studying and chilling'. Marcus would come through every

few nights and spend a couple hours, then he'd roll out. On the most boring of nights I'd log into

facebook to see what was happening with everyone, including the Mrs. She still seemed like the

happy-go-lucky wife that she always was. Marcus was good at hiding his infidelity. He'd play the

good boy, attentive husband roll when responding to her posts. She had the life with him that I

wish I had, only she had it first.

Often times I'd find myself wondering what I was doing dealing with a married man who made it known that he could take or leave our relationship. Then I'd look around at my place, think about my new Benz and my bank account and answer *'Surviving.'*

After a long night of studying and writing, I dozed off on the couch in front of my laptop.

A few hours later I was awakened by the sound of Marcus' ring tone

"Hello?" I asked answering the phone.

"What's up, what you doing'?" He asked.

"I had fallen asleep on the couch. What's up?" I asked rubbing my eyes.

"Trish is on her way over there with some evening gowns, and I have a hairstylist coming an hour after that. Make sure you're ready. We got a party to go to tonight." He said.

"But Marcus I have an exam tomorrow." I pleaded, knowing that he wasn't too fond of me going to school to begin with.

"Slim, if you ain't ready for the shit yet, you never will be. Don't fake on me tonight, I come first, that's why you get all first class shit." He said.

"Really Marcus, so I'm just a slave to you?" I asked upset, not even caring about the argument that was about to ensue.

"Look, I ain't got time for this shit, I got some business to take care of, you rolling' or not?" He asked.

"yeah, fine, whatever, I'll be ready." I said with a sigh.

"I'll be by to scoop you around eight-thirty." He said.

"Fine." I replied.

"I holla." He said then he hung up the phone.

I got up to clean my school things out of the living room. It was tough being owned.

About half an hour later I heard a knock on the door. I looked at the monitor to see that it was Trisha standing outside my door.

"Hey girl." I said after opening the door to let her in.

"Hey lady, aright, I got six dresses for you. I only brought six because these are the six baddest dresses I got." She said as she unzipped the rack to reveal the dresses. She wasn't lying, they looked like something worn to an awards show.

"Damn!" I said looking at the dresses.

"Yes girl, the least expensive dress here is $150,000." She said as she opened the bottom racks to reveal the shoes.

"Get the fuck outta here! What the hell?" I exclaimed. To a poor girl like me, that was a lot of money.

"Uh uh, don't do that! They hate when you act excited over money." Trish said as she shook her head holding up a finger.

"How in the fuck am I not supposed to be shocked? $150,000! I probably never even had that if you combined all the money I had in my whole life." I said.

"See, that's the shit right there that you need to keep to yourself." She said.

"What you mean?" I asked wondering if I was gonna have to rock her ass.

She sat on the edge of the couch and crossed her legs.

"Angel, do you like living like this? Do you enjoy this lifestyle that you're living?" She asked calmly.

"I mean, its good, I've never lived better." I answered.

"Then what you don't want to do, is go around breaking rules. Keep playing your part." She replied.

"I'm not following what you saying? What rules? What part?" I asked.

"Their rules, don't get excited over money, when at an event, don't speak unless your escort invites you into a conversation. Don't challenge what they say, especially not in public. Don't fraternize with people who make less than them.. don't.."

"Wait, what? How in the hell would I know who makes less than them?" I asked feeling that these rules were doing way too much.

"Angel, *everybody* makes less than them. But that mostly means, don't fraternize with the hustlers, lifestyles or the fellas. Them, or their chicks." She said as she stood to her feet to walk back over to the clothing.

I watched her match up shoes with different dresses as she sort of talked to herself about the way they looked together. She must have thought I was done with this convo, but I was far from done.

I knew that she knew more than she let on. The only problem was, I couldn't tell if she were afraid to tell or just didn't want to, but I intended to find out.

"Deytwon has been coming for me, and Marcus keeps getting mad at me when he sees us talk."I said breaking the silence. She looked up at the ceiling and sighed before shaking her head. Then she went back to the clothing.

"You hear me? Deytwon is making it clear that he wants me." I said a little louder.

"Angel, please don't bring me in this shit. I don't want to know shit." She said not looking at me.

"What shit?" I asked.

"Their shit! I don't want to know, I don't want to be involved, I only wanna dress you, and dip the fuck out." She exclaimed.

"Why you getting all extra though? I'm just trying to make conversation." I lied.

"No, you're trying to pump me for information. I told you before, the less you know, the better off you are. They are above the law, you're playing a dangerous game and I want no parts." She said

"That's why I need to know what the fuck is going on! I met a nigga, he was cool and had some good dick! Now he brought me in this world and I have no idea whats going on, but you do, and you wont hip me?" I exclaimed.

"Look, Angel, all I can tell you is to be careful. Think clearly and make the right decision. When I tell you they are above the law, take that shit for all that you think it could mean. You remember that movie the Untouchables?" She asked.

"Not really, I remember my grandmother watching' a black and white show called The Untouchables, though." I said.

"yeah, well they are the real untouchables, except they aren't gangstas." She explained.

"Then what makes them untouchable?" I asked.

"Power, their money is powerful across the globe." She said.

"What the fuck? If they had that kinda bread, why they live in the DMV?" I asked in full doubt.

"Have you ever been to or seen Marcus' house?" She asked.

"No, we use to go to hotels." I replied.

"Right, that's because neither of them actually live here. They buy up land and live on it when they're in town." She said.

"How did they get their money?" I asked wondering if she knew.

Trish looked at me and rolled her eyes.

"If I'm in some deep shit, the least you can do is tell me how deep it is." I said taking her arm.

She shook her head and sat on the back of the couch and took a long deep breath.

"Look, legend is Marcus and Deytwon's great great great grandfathers saved the slave masters daughter and grandson from being run over by a train. After that he took care of them, and when he died he left them a diamond mine and and a gold mine in Africa. But they couldn't read so they didn't know what it was or what to do with it. They stored the deed in some boxes that were later found by one of their great grandsons. He told the other, and they claimed ownership. Its said that there were three men, but no one knows what happened to the third one.

But the three started the Big Boys organization back when they were slaves, but it wasn't until they got the money that they were able to make power moves. They invested a lot of the money and made it grow, now they're a power entity headed by Marcus and Deytwon." She explained.

"OK but.." I started but she cut me off.

"I've already told you too much. That's the last I'm speaking on it." She said holding her hand up in the air.

"But you ain't tell me shit, all you told me was the history, you ain't tell me how they became powerful, how much weight they hold." I said.

"*MONEY*, Angel! Their money is their power. Now please, can you come and pick a dress so that I can roll?" She shouted, out of frustration.

"Yeah whatever, give me the red one with the silver shoes." I said with a sigh.

"Do you know how to tango?" She asked.

"What?" I asked confused.

"Do you know how to dance the tango?" She asked again.

"Uh, no." I replied sarcastically

"Then don't choose that one. This is a dress built specifically for that dance." She said.

"That makes no sense." I replied with a chuckle.

"Not to a chick from the hood." She retorted.

"Watch it shawty, because I am *ALL HOOD*." I said standing to my feet.

"Save it, I'm only here to help. Why don't you try on the black one." She asked taking the black one off the rack. It was a very sexy halter top style form fitting dress with a thigh high split.

"yeah, aright, give me those shoes that strap up my leg to go with these." I said pointing at the shoes I wanted.

"That works." She said reaching in for the shoes.

I went back to the bathroom to try the clothes on. I looked in the mirror and damn near fell in love with myself.

"Damn." I said as I stared at myself

"Hows it coming?" Trish called out from the living room.

I opened the door and walked out into the living room. When she saw me her mouth dropped open and she stood to her feet.

"If you look at another dress, I swear to god I will burn these bitches right now." She said.

"This is the dress." I said.

"That's the dress." She replied.

After I took the dress off I hopped in the shower just to freshen up so that when the stylist got there, she could get to work and then I could be dressed and ready for Marcus.

Trish wanted to stay to make sure the girl doing my hair would do justice to the dress.

My dress was five-hundred thousand, and my accessories, with my shoes included came to one hundred-thousand. I was definitely going to look like some serious money tonight, and I loved it.

It took the girl all of two hours to style my hair. I ended up with an up-do with falling curls. The girl whose name was Fatima was a boss with them hair skills, she wasn't Karen, but a beast no less.

Both Trish and Fatima who knew one another from many appointments like this, wanted to see the finished product. Normally I didn't entertain bitches, but seeing how I was feeling all squeally and girly, I didn't mind them wanting to see their finished product.

I went into my bedroom and undressed. I rubbed lotion on my entire body, then I dabbed scented oil in various places, mainly on pulse points.

Once I finished making sure I smelled sexy, it was time to dress sexy. I starting with my silky black thong, and matching bra. Luckily the dress was of thick enough material where my ass wouldn't be making an imprinted appearance. Then I slipped into my dress and once again found myself staring into the mirror. I could not believe the woman looking back at me, she looked so elegant, so fancy, like a star.

"Oh, I am a star." I said to myself before stepping into my shoes. I fastened the straps around my calf then headed out of the room.

"Girl, I got Ms. Morgan tomorrow, you know how she is, she complain about everything, but she always request me." Fatima said just as Trish tapped her arm to tell her to turn around.

"What yall think?" I asked

"See, that's why I do this shit! You badd as shit slim!" Fatima said as she balled her fist and put it to her mouth.

Trish just stared on in awe like she hadn't just seen me in this dress just a couple hours ago.

"Why you just looking like that?" I asked.

"Cause you winning like shit. You've found your look, you got it." She said.

"Thanks yall, yall both hooked me up like shit." I said.

"Girl, that's what we do. You just go do what you do!" Fatima said.

Trish walked over to me with a small pouch in her hand.

"You don't need make-up, but let me bring out your eyelashes some, hold still." She said as she dipped her hand inside the pouch to retrieve the mascara.

She gently brushed the mascara brush through my eyelashes a couple times. Then she stood back and looked at me.

"Girl!" She said shaking her head.

"Yesssssssss!" Fatima said as we heard the door being unlocked.

We all turned to look at the door until we saw Marcus walk through wearing a black suit under an overcoat that was draped with a long black scarf. He was looking like a million bucks.

"Damn shawty, oh what's up, yall still here?" He said looking from me to them.

"Yeah, we were just leaving!" Trish said as she jumped up and started packing her things.

"She *badd*, right?" Fatima asked Marcus with a soft touch to his arm.

"I only do badd, feel me?" He said smiling at her.

"Mmhmm." She said before going to gather her things.

"Where are your diamonds?" He asked as he approached me.

"Oh, I forgot." I said turning to head towards my room. I went into my jewelry box and grabbed my long diamonds earrings. Then I put on the necklace and bracelet before returning to the living room.

94

When I got there I saw Marcus holding the door open with his hand for Fatima who was leaning up against it talking and returning his smile.

"So you ready?" I asked to interrupt them.

"Yeah, lets be out." Marcus said as he removed his hand from the door. He walked over to the couch to grab my shawl.

"So where is this place we're going?" I asked as he put the shawl over my shoulders.

"We're taking a helicopter out to a Yacht that's sitting on the Potomac." He said as we walked towards the door.

"What?" I asked

"Look, I need you to get into character, all that saying' what, slang and cussing' is out for tonight. Got me?" He asked before opening the door.

"Yes." I replied rolling my eyes into the air.

When we got outside there was a stretch limo parked in front of the building with the chauffeur standing outside.

"Nice." I said as we walked over to the limo.

"Thank you sir." Marcus said as the chauffeur opened the door for us. I stepped inside and moved over to the seats in front of the bar.

"Hmm, may I have a drink?" I asked as Marcus slid into the limo.

"That's cool, just don't get drunk" He said as he started fixing me a drink.

"Now why would I do that?" I asked with a smile as I took the glass from him.

"Yeah, aright." He replied sliding back into his seat. I watched him take out his cell as the driver pulled off.

We rode around for about thirty minutes until we came to a field where there were several

95

helicopters sitting waiting for passengers. We got out of the limo and walked over to the one with Marcus' initials on it.

"You ready to fly?" He asked as the door was opened.

"I thought we were fly." I replied with a flirtatious smile.

"No lie, you know this." He replied as he helped me into the helicopter.

I was a little nervous because I had never flown before, and it was a helluva thing for my first flying experience to be in a helicopter. We flew over the water for a good twenty minutes before we came to a very large yacht that had an X on top.

"Wow, that boat is huge!" I said looking down at the lights.

"yeah, because its a Yacht." Marcus replied as we started our descent down.

When we got onto the yacht the door to the helicopter was opened and we were helped off. We were escorted down to the lower level where we heard the helicopter take flight again.

"Hey how you doing', boss?" Marcus asked a man wearing a suit and white gloves.

"Hello Mr. Jones, welcome aboard." The man replied.

"So you need to run to the restroom or anything or you good?" Marcus asked me.

"How my hair look?" I asked

"Flawless." He replied.

"Then I'm good." I replied smiling hard.

"We're ready." Marcus said to the man in the suit and white gloves

We followed him through the yacht to another lower level where everyone was. There was a live band playing behind a wooden dance floor.

Groves of people were there, some dancing, some standing around by the railing, others standing in groups talking. The tables made a semi circle around the dance floor and stretched all

96

the way back to the other end of the large space. The lights on this level were dim as to not overpower the beautiful night sky. One thing about Marcus and his team, they knew what it meant to go all out.

"My man, what's good?" Asked a guy who walked over to us.

"Hey dude, what's going on?" Marcus asked as they slapped hands.

"Shit, chilling',chilling', loving' this good life." The guy replied.

"No doubt. Well look, let me get in a seat, I'ma get up with you when we take them shots." Marcus said.

"Bet that." The guy said just before we walked away.

"Can I ask you a question?" I asked as the man in the suit and white gloves approached a table.

"Not if its gonna blow me." He said as he pulled out my seat for me.

"It might." I replied.

"Then don't. Thank you sir, you've been of great assistance." Marcus said as he shook the man in the suit with the white gloves hand.

"No, thank you sir, for allowing me to assist you." The waiter replied with a big smile.

"This man right here!" Said some guy approaching Marcus before he could sit down.

"Aw shit, whats good man? You ain't been coming through, you been good?" Marcus asked as he and the guy shook hands

"Nah, yeah, you know me and the wife just getting back from Italy, she wanted to take a cooking class over there, so we went for a month." The guy explained.

"What better way right?" Marcus replied.

"No doubt, we had a ball too. I learned to speak a lil Italian and all that." The guy said.

"Yeah, Tiff and I were there last summer. She ain't care for it too much so we only stayed about a week." Marcus said. I hated when he mentioned his wife in front of me.

At that moment I turned my attention towards the people in the room. There weren't quite as many people as there were at the restaurant, but there were still quite a few. As my eyes continued their voyage around the room I noticed most people, including the women were laughing it up and having a good time.

In the midst of all the laughing faces, my eyes fell upon a pair of eyes staring at me. They belonged to a medium complexioned woman. Her hair was swooped up into a sloppy bun on top of her head and she was wearing a silver pop collar dress. She stared on at me with a look that told me she knew me and she didn't fuck with me. I gritted on her (disrespectful look), and she looked away. She did look somewhat familiar but I didn't know where I could possibly know her from. I had no know beef with any chick at the moment.

I glanced back over to see her staring at me again giving me the same look as she slowly shook her head. Trying hard to respect Marcus' rules, I gave the bitch a head nod then turned my attention elsewhere. I knew that if it were like that, I would see the bitch again in a more appropriate setting to deliver her the ass whuppin' she was so desperately seeking.

"Hey, I'm bout to step off real quick, make yourself comfortable, you don't need an escort here, just don't do nothing' stupid." Marcus said as he leaned in and whispered into my ear.

"So what should I do?" I asked still a lil heated from the moment I just had with the chick across the room.

"Whatever you want, you're the girl on Marcus' arm, this yacht is your oyster." He said stepping off before I could ask anymore questions. Not wanting to be bored all night, I stood to my feet and looked around. There was the dance floor, but I wasn't really feeling the band all like that. There was the bar, but Marcus asked me not to get drunk. That's when I noticed a snack table.

"Jackpot." I said as I made my way over to the table.

"Good evening madam, how are you on this fine evening?" The server asked as I approached the table.

"I'm great." I replied reaching for a small dish. The man took it before I could grab it.

"Tell me what you would like madam, and I will serve you." He said with a wide grin.

"I guess, some of that cheese, a couple crackers, and a few strawberries." I said

"Excellent madam, here you are, please enjoy." He said handing me the small dish.

"Thank you." I replied with a smile before walking away.

I walked the floor for a few seconds before noticing an empty space over at the railing. I loved looking at the water at night, and from the yacht the view was quite beautiful.

I stood there and looked as far out across the water as I could. The sky was very dark out over the water so it was hard to see the horizon. The reflection of the moon danced along the waves as they bounces and crashed against one another. I was so mesmerized by how sexy nature could be when left to its own devices.

"Beautiful view, isn't it?" I heard Deytwon's voice from behind.

In lieu of a reply I nodded my head and continued to look on.

"I see a view like this every night, I have to, its the only way to maintain my sanity." He said now standing beside me.

"That sounds like a sad life. Well, anyway, gotta go." I said turning to leave.

"Do you?" He asked as I turned to leave.

"Yes, he does not like me talking to you, and I don't like him when he doesn't like something." I replied.

"He hurts you?" Deytwon asked.

"No, he doesn't hurt me. Just, please, leave me alone." I said before quickly walking away.

I found my way back over to my table where I sat resting my chin on my hand.

"Madam, would you like to order anything to eat or drink?" A waiter asked after approaching the table.

"Yes, may I have a glass of wine, any wine." I asked trying to calm my nerves. I knew that Marcus saw me speaking with Deytwon and there was no telling what he would do about that tonight.

"Yes madam." The waiter said before walking away. I glanced around the room until i spotted Marcus. He was sitting on the upper deck at a table with a group of men and a few females. They were drinking and talking it up having a good old time. I shook my head not believing that he left me to go chill with some other people, knowing that I knew no one here.

I sat at the table feeling bored and quite stupid. Why would he bring me here to carry me like this? Every since I moved into the condo he was becoming even more neglectful and careless in the way that he treated me. It was as though he knew that I needed him and wasn't going anywhere, no matter what. I shook my head and tried to redirect my thoughts. No need to feel sorry for myself if I wasn't going to do anything about it.

I looked back over at the railing to see if Deytwon was still there, and he wasn't. Though once again, I found Ms. Eyes looking at me with the same lil attitude she had on her face the first two times. I rolled my eyes at her and looked away. I didn't have time for that bitch shit, not right now when there was nothing that I could do about it.

About thirty minutes later Marcus came back to the table cheerfully as though he never left, or saw nothing wrong with leaving me alone for so long.

"Hey shawty, what's good, you eat something?" He asked still laughing at whatever he found funny on his way back to the table.

"Nah, I'm not hungry." I replied dryly

"yeah, I can see that you're full on attitude. Let me know if I need to remind you that this ain't the place for all that." He replied

"Why do you bring me here, to leave me alone?" I asked quietly.

"Slim, these events are fun for the folks who don't know no better. These are business meetings for me. I'm taking care of business." He said.

"yeah, I saw you laughing it up with your associates up on the upper deck." said before taking a sip.

"I saw something too, you wanna discuss that now?" He asked as he leaned into me giving the appearance that he was being loving.

I shot a look at him as I swallowed the champagne.

"That was.." I started but he stopped me.

"Nothing, yeah, I know, it never is, right?" He asked with a chuckle as he signaled for the waiter.

"Who am I here with?" I asked trying to play the loyalty card.

"Me, I brought you." He replied with a shrug.

"Who am I leaving with?" I asked.

"You tell me. Good evening sir, could I trouble you for a cigar?" Marcus asked the waiter when he approached the table.

"Of course sir, it would be my pleasure." The waiter said before walking away.

"If I came with you, I'm leaving with you. You have been the only one for as long as we've been knowing each other. Why are you coming at me like you have to question your position?" I asked quietly.

"Shawty, I know my position in life, that's the only position that mean anything to me. I'm just not for the games and the lies." He said.

"I've never lied to you." I said.

"Never say never, I hate that word." He replied before he stood to his feet. He retrieved the cigar from the waiter who then lit it for him.

"Thanks boss." Marcus said as he shook the waiters hand.

"My pleasure sir, thank you" The waiter replied before stepping off.

"So you plan to ignore and avoid me for the rest of the night?" I asked.

Marcus turned around and looked down at me but didn't reply.

"I see you've left your seat again." I said.

"What don't you have that you really need right now? Before you answer that, think about what you do have, a boss ass place to stay, a bad ass car, free money, and you in school now. What you lacking'?" He asked.

"What's the recount for?" I asked.

"I'm just trying to make sense out of your beef." He said after taking a pull.

"You've stood up Marcus, what are you about to go do right now that requires me to be alone again?" I asked.

"Handle some business, and I'd think you'd appreciate that, seeing' how you're wearing more money on you right now, than the average nigga make in a year." He said.

"Touche'." I replied tired of going back and forth over a point that will never be made or understood,

"Order something, eat, drink, it'll all be over soon." He said with a smile and a wink.

I shook my head as I watched him walk away. I couldn't tell if it were Marcus who was changing, or if he were just being revealed to me. He made it no secret that he could care less about me, even when I made it no secret how much I did care about him.

He was starting to make me feel owned and that I should realize and appreciate it. It gave me a very eerie feeling and I didn't like it at all. I watched as he was stopped along his path to "handle business" to speak with every guy along the way. The women watched him too, he was a highly attractive man and his appeal was on a thousand when he wore a suit.

I turned around in my chair to find something else to do in order to keep busy while I wait for his 'gracious return'. That's when I saw the chick watching me again. I was in a mind set that encouraged me to walk up on her to find out what was really good, but since I didn't know the consequences of breaking the rules in this kind of setting, I fell back and memorized her face. If she stayed in the city, I knew that I would see her again.

*****

## Chapter 10

### Angel

Marcus and I stayed on the yacht for a few of the longest most boring hours I have ever experienced in my life. Finally it was time to leave so we were escorted on to the top deck where our helicopter sat waiting for us. We flew back to land in complete silence. Once we landed we were escorted back to our limo where our driver was waiting outside by the backdoor.

"Look, I got one more appearance to make, then you can go home and chill out for the night." Marcus said once the door was closed.

"Fine." I replied looking down at my nails.

He smirked as he took out his cell and started scrolling. I shook my head and turned my attention to the street. Again we rode in silence and this time, I really didn't care.

It didn't take long for us to arrive at our destination, which was the Grand Hyatt Hotel in DC.

A doorman ran up and opened the door to the limo to let us out.

"Good evening sir, welcome to the Grand Hyatt hotel." He said as Marcus and I stepped out of the limo.

"Thank you sir, quick service, I love it." Marcus said as he shook the mans hand.

"My pleasure sir, thank you for allowing me to serve you." The doorman replied.

Marcus took my arm and escorted me inside the hotel, where we were then escorted into a large banquet hall.

"Our table is over there, I just need to sign a paper, then we will leave. We are not staying at this event, do not get comfortable." He instructed.

"Fine." I replied just as I noticed my left earring wasn't dangling like that right. I touched my ear and realized the earring had come out.

"Oh my gawd!" I said.

'What?!" Marcus asked irritated.

"My earring, I lost it." I said looking around on the floor beside us.

"And?" he asked.

"And, its a damn diamond earring." I said letting go of his arm.

"Slim, you really gonna do this now? You really about to get bent over an earring?" He asked

"A diamond earring, you damn right." I said.

"Shawty, an earring is and earring. If its that much a part of your pulsation process, I'll get you another pair." He said.

"I have to go check outside." I said ignoring him.

"Just go wait in the limo." He said as he walked away from me.

I looked at him for a moment not believing that he just walked away from me like '*fuck you.'*

"Fuck that." I said as I turned to leave. I went outside and looked around for the earring. It was nowhere to be found. Finally I just gave up. I looked at the long line of limos on the street and tried to remember which one was ours. That's when I heard a pair of heels walking up behind me. I turned around to see the bitch from the yacht standing before me.

"Fuck you want?" I asked with my attitude on full blast.

"You hear wit Marcus, ain't you?" She asked sounding like a purebred hood-rat.

"Yup, fuckin him and all that, what's it to you?" I replied rocking my neck.

"Skank bitch! That's my best friends husband!" She exclaimed as she charged me.

"THANK YOU!" I exclaimed as I caught her in the face with a right hook. I was ready to relieve myself of this anger that's been mounting in me for sometime. She stumbled off to the side, but was able to catch herself before she fell.

"BITCH IMA KILL YOU BITCH, YOU DEAD AS SHIT BITCH!" She screamed as she ran towards me with her fist.

While she went windmill, I went punching bag, tagging the shit out of her face. She reached and grabbed my hair and tried to yank me but I just kept tagging her. Little did she know I grew up fighting niggas and bitches and wasn't no slouch at the shit by far.

Eventually I got tired and yanked her ass to the ground and straddled her while close fist slapping the shit out of her. I didn't even hear the cops pull up, but I felt them as they grabbed me and pull me up off of her.

"You dead bitch, you is dead! Fuck you trifling bitch, fuckin another woman's husband! Dirty bitch!" She screamed through bloody swollen lips.

"You want me? Any of your bitches want me? Come see about me, I live in Georgetown! I ain't hard to find bitch, I'm the only black chick out there!" I exclaimed as the cop pushed me away from her.

"Alright, calm all the shit the fuck down! The fuck is going on here? Calm her ass down over there?" A cop asked once I was up against his car.

"Officer, I was in there with my man, and I lost a earring so I came out here to find it. Then she came up to me, talking' shit, and she started swinging on me!" I exclaimed.

"That's a damn lie, you came for me! I ain't even do shit!" She shouted from across the way.

"Oh, you did shit, you got yo ass whupped!" I shouted back.

"yeah yeah, yall both going' in. Talk about it in the holding tank." The third cop said after he collected our things from the ground.

"Let's just read 'em their rights and lets get the fuck out of here. These swanky people annoy men" Said the cop that was holding the other chick.

"Look, my man is in there, can somebody just go get him?" I asked thinking that Marcus could get me off.

"He's in there, but you out here acting like a hoodie, yeah, I believe that." The cop said as he turned me around.

"I'm not a hood rat, I was defending myself." I said

"Yet she's the one all fucked up."The cop replied with a chuckle.

"I don't play no games." I said.

"Neither do I.. you have the right to remain silent.." The officer started reading me my rights as he cuffed me.

<><><><>

## Deytwon

My limo pulled up to the Grand Hyatt just in time to see Angels head being guided into the police car. I looked around for Marcus but he was nowhere in sight. The nosy crowd of people were beginning to disperse as their entertainment was driven away.

"Excuse me beautiful, can you tell me what happened here?" I called out to one of two ladies who were walking by, after letting down my window. They both turned to look with the coldest mug on their faces until they saw me in my limo.

"Oh, uhm, there was a fight. Two women were going at it hard." One of the ladies explained.

"The police broke it up and just took them away." The other chimed in.

"Wow, that must've been crazy huh?" I asked signaling to the chauffeur that I was ready to get out.

"Yes, it was wild. They were out here looking' like they going' to the prom or something, rolling around in their dresses." The first lady said.

"yeah, that is wild. Well, thank you ladies, you two be safe out here and enjoy your night." I said as the chauffeur opened the door for me.

"So, uh, what's your name?" The first lady asked.

"My name is Deytwon, and before this goes any further, I must tell you, my heart is already taken. Good evening ladies" I said with a wink before walking by them into the hotel.

"Damn, probably with some dopey white girl." I heard one of the ladies mutter.

"Fuck it lets go." The other said.

When I stepped inside the banquet hall I scanned the room for Marcus. I spotted him talking with a guy named Dave and his side chick Leonda. Marcus didn't seem to realize that Angel was missing or perhaps he didn't care. She has never been out of his sight that I have seen since he first started bringing her around, so this was a little odd. I wondered if he knew that she had been arrested.

When he noticed me looking he raised his glass at me. I in turn nodded my head towards him.

"Good evening Mr. Richards. Is there anything that I can get for you?" Asked a server.

"Yes, actually, could you get me a pen and pad please?" I asked as I slipped a bill into his pocket.

"Of course sir, right away sir." He said as he eagerly went on his way.

"Rich, hows it going?" Asked Bill, a top level Big Boy.

"Good as always, how about you, how are you and Tyra?" I asked as we slapped hands.

"I'm good and she's perfect so we're great!" He said with a chuckle.

"Right, right." I replied as the server returned with the pen and pad.

"Is there anything else that you require sir?" He asked as I began scribbling a note on the pad.

"Yes, if you will so kindly pass this to Mr. Jones, you will have exceeded my expectations for an excellent evening." I said.

"Thank you sir, I will do my best." He replied.

"That's why you're here my good man." I said sliding him another hundred.

"So when we going' see you with some arm candy at one of these things?" Bill asked once the server left.

"You see this? This is the only type of arm candy I'm interested in." I said lifting my sleeve to show off my Diamond Rolex.

"Man, I'm trying to be like you when I grow up" Bill said with a chuckle.

I shook my head.

"That's that jealous nigga shit right there. Jealous niggas joke about what's seriously on their heart. Then they become a problem." I said. Bills face got tight for a second then it filled with humor.

"Aw man you like the *show off*." He said.

"Let me help you out. I've been raised on standard. I won't live below those standards, so to a person who doesn't have my standards or the means to live my standards, yeah, I appear to like the show off. But to the man who knows better, I'm just doing' me, living my life.

"Every things a life lesson with you man." Bill said before sipping his drink.

"Each one teach one so we all can grow." I explained.

"No doubt, but you gotta admit, your man Marcus is a show off. Even he says it himself." Bill said.

I glanced over at Marcus who had just shot my note into the trash like a basketball.

"Yeah, my nigga for life, likes to be seen." I said as he looked back at me and shrugged.

I chuckled to myself as I shook my head. I knew then that he had no intentions on getting her out.

"Aright man I need to go make a phone call, be easy." I said as I slapped hands with Bill. I stepped outside and took out my phone to call Trisha.

****

## Chapter 11

### Angel

When we got down to the precinct, I was booked, questioned and searched. Then they put me in a holding cell with other women who were still in street clothing. I felt so stupid sitting there in a damn evening gown, with my hair all over my head, and wearing one earring.

"Angel?" I heard a chick say my name. I looked up to see my girl Leslie who I hadn't seen in a few years. She was one of my best friends that I had lost touch with. The girl was crazy as shit, always down for whatever, whenever.

"Aw damn, what's up Lee lee?" I asked as I stood up to meet her halfway.

"Giiiirlah.. what the fuck you doing' in here?" She asked hugging me.

"Whuppin' a bitches ass. What you doing' in here?" I asked once we let go.

"I stabbed Toddy's bitchass, they brings me down here and takes this nigga to the hospital. You can see that bitch nigga hit me right? So why the fuck am I in here for self defense?" She asked pointing to her black eye.

"The fuck you mean he hit you? Where they do that shit at?" I asked surprised that her baby father put his hands on her. He never gave off the impression that he was that type of nigga to me.

"yeah that bitch nigga hit me, so I stabbed him. I was going for his chest but he moved so I hit his arm. He thought I was fuckin' playing', this nigga saw me, but he didn't believe me. I'm crazy!" She said.

"Oh I know that shit, but damn, you OK though? He ain't dead is he?" I asked.

"Girl fuck no, he good, I ain't hit nothing' major, like I was trying too. But anyway, fuck that bitch, who in the fuck was you fighting'?" She asked.

"Girl I don't know, some bitch call herself rushing' me. Talking' some dumbshit, so I had to let her have it." I said hitting my fist.

"Bet that shit, gotta let these bitches know, it ain't a game. Fighting' was life growing up, if we didn't know shit else, we knew how to whup a mufucka's ass." She said with a laugh.

"No doubt." I replied.

"Shiiiit, so how Salisha doing? She marry that bum ass nigga yet? He ain't got shit, don't own shit, but she in love." Leslie said.

"Nah, they just moved in together though, they doing' their thing." I said.

"Well shit, if she like it, I love it. What about you, where you stay now?" She asked.

"Out G'town." I replied

"Get the fuck outta here." She said surprised.

"For a few months now." I said.

"Oh my gawd, why do bitches lie?" She asked.

"Bitch please, lie to you for what?" I asked.

"How you do that though?" She asked.

"Long ass story, but its legit. Yeah. I'm in school now and everything." I said.

"School? Where you go?" She asked.

"UDC." I replied.

"Bitch, University of Dumb Children, that ain't no school." She said laughing

"Fuck you. Its an accredited college, and I'm getting my credits to get my degree. I'm doing' me." I replied.

"I feel you, do your thing. Nah, you know that's what they use to call it back in the day, its all love bitch, don't get in ya feelings." She said.

"Anyway, what you got going' on trick?" I asked hating how people always rag on UDC, even to this day.

"Shit, just my nigga and my kid. You know I drive the buses now." She said.

"Aw shit, you work for Metro? That's whats up." I said.

"yeah, I've been with them for like six months now, it pays the bills. So I'm straight with or without a nigga." She said.

"No doubt, that's how it should be." I replied wishing that my own situation would reflect such.

"Powers, come make your call!" I heard a guard call out my name.

"Aright chick, I be back." I said as I turned to walk through the cell door.

"Phone over there, you got ten minutes." The guard said. I walked over to the desk and took up the phone and immediately dialed Marcus' number..

### Marcus

So that bitch got herself locked up, serves her right. Fuck she mean by chasing behind diamonds while on *my* arm. Tried to make me look foolish, now you look stuck. I chuckled to myself as I watched Deytwon leave the banquet hall. No doubt he was about to get her out and clean it up. Nigga ain't even had the pussy and already he's whipped.

I shook my head at the thought. Never will a bitch ever have me like that, and I love my wife.

Angel was pretty, very easy on the eyes, especially when looking into her soft brown eyes. A soft nigga could fall weak. Her body was thick and her sex was gangsta. She was a bad bitch all around, but without experiencing even half of that, Deytwon was on her like a crackhead. I almost felt like it was all a game to show me up. Love don't even run this deep, or does it?

Twenty minutes later I felt my phone vibrate against my chest. I took it out to see an un-programmed 202 number flashing across the screen.

"Yo." I said but was greeted by a recording about a collect call from jail

*'Guess Deytwon didn't go get her out after all.'* I thought to myself with a chuckle.

"Aye Marcus, we bout to head up to the penthouse for the after party, you rolling?" Paul asked as I was stepping off.

"yeah, I'll be up. Tell 'em save the Brazilian for me, don't nobody touch her.... yeah I'll accept the charges." I said as I walked out of the banquet hall.

## Angel

"The fuck you doing' calling me from jail slim?" Marcus asked once we were cleared to talk.

"Some bitch from the event walked up on me when I was outside, she asked me if I was with you, then she said you were her best friends husband and she rushed me." I explained.

"What the fuck?" He asked.

"Yes, so you know who she is?" I asked.

"I might." He replied.

"OK, it don't even matter right now. Can you please come down here and get me out? Please? I don't want to spend the night here!" I said.

"Look, I'm in the middle of a very important meeting, I'll be there when I can, aright." He said.

"Marcus." I said not believing that he wasn't making my emergency his priority.

"Angel, my life don't stop just 'cause you made a bad decision." He said.

"Bad decision? What was I supposed to do, let her beat me?" I asked.

"You were supposed to not trip so hard about losing an earring. You were supposed to be on my arm while I handled my business. Instead you made me look like a cheap nigga running around with a chick that thought she lost the last pair of diamonds on earth." He said.

"You aren't coming, are you?" I asked after a long sigh. I was now near tears as I was starting to see for the first time, to what extent that he really didn't give a damn about me.

"Like I said, I'll be there when I can." He said.

"OK" I replied feeling completely defeated.

**"I holla." He said.**

**"Goodbye Marcus." I said before hanging up the phone.**

I closed my eyes and fought back the tears as hard as I could. I decided that I would not shed another tear for that nigga. It was time to shed my feelings for him and take the shit for what it really was. I had no place to go, so I knew that I'd have to play his game until I could come up on my own. I hated myself for giving up everything to rely on him, but we live and we learn.

I was escorted back to the holding cell where Leslie and I talked until we fell asleep on one another. I was awakened to the sound of someone shouting my name..

**"POWERS! GET UP, LETS GO, You made bail!" I heard a guard scream.**

**"Thank you Marcus." I said as I sat up to stretch..**

## Deytwon

"Thanks for doing this on such short notice." I said to Trisha as she handed me the gift wrapped box. I had her meet me at the Police Station where Angel was being held.

"Never a problem for you." She said with a flirtatious smile.

"So how you been?" I asked

"I've been good, chilling, about to open a boutique soon." She said proud.

"That's what's up, you need a backer or you good?" I asked.

"Nah, I'm straight, I've been saving so I'm able to do it all on my own." She said.

"OK, OK, I see you. Well congratulations." I said giving her a slight hug.

"Thanks Deytwon." She replied embracing me.

"Well look, let me go handle this business, if you need anything, some strings pulled or anything to that effect, holla at me." I said.

"I will, bye Dey." She said smiling before walking over to her car just as the limo I ordered pulled up.

I walked over to the driver to give him my instructions.

"Hello, I'm Deytwon, you're Paul?" I asked

"Yes sir." He replied stepping out of the limo.

"OK, Paul, so what's going to happen is you're going to transport a woman by the name of Angel to this address. She's going to go in, I want you to wait for her to come back, no matter what she says. If she doesn't come back out in thirty minutes give me a call on this number on the back of the card." I said handing him the card.

"OK, sir." The driver said taking the card.

"Open the door so that I can put this on the seat in the back." I said.

Paul walked over and opened the back door after taking the box from me to place on the seat.

"Good, I will be back." I said as he closed the door.

I walked inside the Police Station and up to the desk.

"Hello, how may I help you?" Asked a lady officer behind the desk.

"Hello beautiful, is the Sargent in?" I asked.

"Yes, handsome, I'll get him for you."she replied blushing all over herself.

A few seconds later a big burly bubble gut man who was missing hair in the middle of his head came out looking like he couldn't believe someone had the nerve to disturb him.

"How are you, I'm Deytwon Richards, may I have a minute of your time?" I asked as I extended my hand for him to shake.

He gritted his mouth,squeezing his lips together as he dragged his eyes down to look at my hand. His eyes grew wide when he saw the Big Boy ring on my finger.

"Sir, its a pleasure to meet you? How may I assist you?" He asked changing his tone.

"Your guys, who were only doing their job, picked up a woman last night for fighting in public. I need her released and her record to be cleared." I said.

"Yes sir, what was her name?" He asked as he walked around behind the desk.

"Angel Powers." I said as I moved closer to the desk.

"Awe yes, I have her file right here. Never before had a criminal record, this will be easy." He said as he walked around gathering information.

"Your woman?" The lady officer behind the desk asked while the Sargent walked around in back.

118

Sidechick Blues The Plot by Nikida Bellezza

"Yes she is." I answered.

"Hmm, lucky her." She spat, rolling her eyes.

"Lucky me." I replied.

"I can make you lucky, alright." She said licking her lips.

"I bet you can, you look like a woman who knows how to do some things, and for the right man, you should." I said.

"Who's to say you're not the right man?" She asked leaning forward on the desk.

"I do." I replied

"Anyway." She said sucking her teeth.

"Here you are sir. I've asked the CO to get her out, she should be out here in a few minutes." The Sargent said handing me Angels file.

"Thank you sir, you have been of great assistance." I said shaking his hand.

He looked down at his hand and back up at me with a huge smile.

"My pleasure." He replied gratefully.

I nodded my head before turning to leave. When I got to the door I noticed that it had started raining. My chauffeur ran over to me with the umbrella to escort me.

"Thank you Milton." I said as we walked back over to the Royce.

"Deytwon!!" I  heard Angel call just before I got into the Royce...

◇◇◇◇

### Angel

"Well aright girl, stay in touch, if this shit don't go south and I get to go home sometime soon, I'ma' be moving back with my grandmother, over there off Benning and Minnesota. You remember." Leslie said after we hugged.

"yeah, I remember, aright I'll stop by there, I ain't seen her in a minute anyway." I said.

"Aright, aright lady, be easy." She said.

"Aright girl." I replied before following the guard out of the cell.

"Go to the desk to collect your things." The guard said when we got back to the front.

I walked over to the desk and stood behind some man who was demanding to see his son.

"The fuck you mean I can't see my boy? Ain't they allowed visits in the muthafucka?" The man shouted.

"You, come over here." Another guard said calling me over to her. I walked over to the counter and looked at her.

"You Powers?" She asked.

"Yeah." I replied.

"Here are your things." She said tossing my bag of things onto the counter like it wasn't shit

"I ain't got to sign for this?" I asked.

She looked up at me with an attitude spinning her neck into half a circle before she spoke.

"Did I *ask* you to sign anything? No, here go your stuff, you are free to go. You were never here. Goodbye." She said all in one breath.

"Mmhmm, never mind." I said taking my things. I didn't need to get into it with a cop I'd

120

never get out of fuckin jail. I turned thinking I would see Marcus in the waiting area, but he was no where to be seen.

"Hey, who got me out?" I asked turning back around to Sargent Bitch.

"Look, some guy came in here and took care of it aright. He just left out like a few seconds ago." She said attitude still on a thousand..

"Whew lawd." I said with a laugh before turning to leave. I jogged out of the station to see if I could catch who it was that let me out. Other than Marcus, no one else knew that I was in here.

I got all the way outside before I saw the Rolls Royce parked in front of the station. Deytwon was just getting into the backseat.

"DEYTWON!" I yelled out to him. His Chauffeur had just closed the umbrella when Deytwon lift his head up to see who was calling him. He said something to the chauffeur who opened the umbrella and covered his head as he stepped back out of the car.

I hadn't even realize it was raining, so I stood there getting soaked as I stared over at Deytwon with nothing to say.

I couldn't believe he had come to get me out of jail. How did he even know that I was there to begin with.

"Go home." I heard him say after a few seconds of us staring back and forth at each other. He tilted his head towards a limo that was parked to the left of me.

The chauffeur of that limo walked over to me with an umbrella and escorted me back over to the limo. I looked over at Deytwon who was getting back in the Royce.

"Madam." My chauffeur said after having opened the door for me.

"Thank you." I replied as I stepped inside the limo. He closed the door behind me and walked around to get into the front.

I got inside the limo where I found a big white box with a huge blue bow wrapped around it. When I opened the box I was shocked to find clothing. Bra, panties, a shirt, jeans, thin black socks and some Christian Dior boots.

"What the hell? But wha..?" I started but by the time I looked back the Rolls Royce was gone. I looked forward towards the chauffeur and noticed that the partition was up. I shook my head and looked back down at the clothing. For the life of me I didn't know what they were for, but I loved the outfit all the same.

Without any help from me, the chauffeur was able to take me home. When I got there I saw a black Audi parked out front with the word KING on the license plate. I had never seen this car, but I knew that it belonged to Marcus. Seeing how he was at the condo, I decided that it would be best to leave the gift in the limo.

The chauffeur opened the door for me and walked me over to the building with the umbrella over my head.

"Is there anything else you require of me madame?" He asked with a slight bow.

"Nah, I'm good, thank you." I replied before turning to go inside.

I walked into my building and took the elevator up to my apartment. Once inside, I slowly walked back to my room where I saw Marcus peering out of the windows.

*****

## Chapter 12

### Angel

"Lovely view of the city, don't you think?" Marcus asked with his back still to me.

"Its aright." I replied with attitude. I was pissed that he hadn't come get me out of jail, yet he was here chilling

"I swear, you can take the bitch out the ghetto." He said with a sick laugh as he turned around to face me.

"Oh yeah, so I'm a bitch now? Is that why you ain't come get me out of jail?" I asked folding my arms.

"I was coming, eventually." He said with a shrug.

"Yeah, no worries, somebody beat you to it!" I exclaimed not worried about the consequences of bringing Deytwon's name into the conversation.

"Yeah, I know, funny, that nigga is always the fuck around, but you not fuckin' him. Or I'm supposed to believe you not." Marcus said now having a seat on the window seal.

"I already told you I'm not. What the fuck do I need to lie to you for? But you know what, it's all good. You can fuckin' have this life, I'm done with all of it. I'm out!" I shouted as I started gathering my things.

"Oh you leaving'? Bet, take this with you!" He said slapping me to the ground after he approached me.

My face stung like hell where he hit me, and before I could catch myself my reflexes kicked in and I swung on him but I missed. He in turned grabbed my arms, turned me around and pushed me up against the wall hard, all in one motion.

"Bitch you got me fucked up. I could cremate you alive and smoke your ashes. Don't you ever swing on me again." He said after closing in on my ear.

"Marcus, please just let me go." I cried struggling under his grip.

"Oh, you can roll. But leave all my shit here. Don't take *shit* that you ain't walk in that door with." He said after letting me out of his grip.

"But, that's everything." I said as I rubbed my shoulder which ached from my arm being bent behind my back,

"That's right, *everything*." He said nodding his head towards me.

When I realized what he was saying my heart immediately dropped. I couldn't believe that he was about to send me out of here ass naked.

"Marcus.." I started, trying to plead with him, but i knew that it was of no use, the sanity had long left his eyes. The bad angel had full authority over him and the last thing I needed was to trigger the snap.

I slowly began to remove my clothing until I was down to my bra and panties. He continued to deliver a cold hard stare as he raised his eyebrow at me as if to say 'keep going'

"Marcus, please." I begged crying new tears.

"Fuck you." He replied slowly.

I shook my head as my mind began to orbit around the fact that I once thought I loved this man. Within seconds that love was transforming into pure hatred.

After I completely removed the panties and bra, Marcus walked passed me and into the foyer where I heard him open the door.

I stood there in the room naked, trying to make sense of the situation. I was hoping that Marcus was only joking, only bluffing that he was going to send me outside naked, just to show me that I was wrong. But my hope was just that, and had no place in this harsh reality.

After a few moments, I took a deep breath and walked out of the room and into the living room area where I saw him leaning on the door holding it open.

I took another deep breath and forced myself to walk through. It was the longest walk of my life. I felt as though I was on my way to be executed. When I got to the door, I looked him in his eyes one last time. He looked up into mines and smiled at me, the kind of evil smile you'd think the devil had. I simply nodded my head and walked out of the door and kept walking as I heard it slam behind me.

My heart began to pound as my blood rushed adrenaline through my veins. I wanted to fall to the floor curl up in a ball and die.

"This can't be life." I said just as I heard a noise in the distance. I ran and hid in a corner, wishing I had made friends with my neighbors so that I could knock on one of their doors to get some clothes. When I heard a door open and close, I ducked out and moved to another corner. This was going to be hard.

The idea was to get outside, but being outside would be far worse. How could a naked woman evade being seen by people. Worse than that, where in the hell would I go? How would I make it back to Southeast to Salisha's apartment, seeing how I didn't have a phone or money to use a payphone.

What the fuck was I going to do? I gave up my home, I had no family, no money, no job, no nothing. I was literally assed out.

"Come on Angel, think, think." I said to myself as my need to survive kicked in. I attempted to wipe away the endless flow of tears that fell from my eyes while trying to conceal as much of my private areas as possible. My full bouncing breast were the hardest to hide, one hand wasn't doing it. But I needed that hand below just as bad.

I couldn't believe Marcus was carrying me like this. He was not this nigga when I met him, or at least he hid the shit well.

The reality of it was, although I never did anything to him to deserve this, I knew that this was karma on full blast. I'm laid up, falling in love with a married man. How did I really think this shit would end, but hell, not like this.

After believing the coast was clear I decided to run for the next corner, only this time I was caught.

"Oh my gawd Hank!" Exclaimed a woman who had just exited her apartment with her boyfriend.

"Holie shit!" Hank shouted causing others to open their doors.

I was mortified to the hundredth power as I ran as fast as i could to get out of the building.

"What the fuck is going on bro?" I heard someone ask as yet another door was opened.

"Dude, naked black chick running around the condo!" I heard a guy shout.

Suddenly I heard a flood of footsteps heading in my direction. I had no choice but to run outside, and so I did at top speed.

When I got outside I saw the limo still sitting out there. The chauffeur had been standing at the back door as though he were waiting for me. When he saw me run out of the building naked, his eyed grew wide and he rushed to open the door.

"Oh my gawd, Cassie look!" I heard a girl say

"Good Lord!" Another woman exclaimed.

I damn near dived into the back seat of the limo and ran to the opposite end. The chauffeur quickly shut the door behind me and rushed around to get into the drivers seat as people started gathering around and pointing at the limo.

Even thought I knew that they could not see me, it sure felt like they could. I hid under the seat until the diver pulled away and we were no longer in their sight.

By this time the adrenaline wore off and I was left with nothing but shame, embarrassment, fear and hurt. These emotions conquered me all at once sending my body into a frenzy. I cried so hard that I started sobbing. I reached for the box of clothing and started trying to put them on. The task was quite difficult because I was shaking and trembling uncontrollably. The tears blurred my vision and my heart thump felt strange. The last thing I remember was stepping into the jeans.

### Deytwon

"Hello?" I asked answering my cell.

"Yes, Mr. Richards, Ms. Angel came back out, but she passed out in the limousine." The chauffeur said sounding panicked.

"Paul, calm down. Where are you located?" I asked calmer than I felt.

"Sir, I'm on Wisconsin Avenue, Northwest." He said.

"OK, I'm not far from the hospital. Meet on on Reservoir rd." I instructed.

"Yes sir." He replied then I disconnected the call.

"Milton, go to Georgetown Hospital." I said pressing the intercom.

"Yes sir." He replied as he switched lanes.

I scrolled through my phone to call the Doctor.

"Dr. Ben." He said answering his phone.

"Ben, this is Rich, I need you asap, can you meet me at the beach house in an hour?" I asked.

"Certainly, I'm on my way now." He said.

"Thank you." I replied before ending the call.

When I got to reservoir rd, I was pleased to see that the limo was already there waiting.

I instructed the Milton to pull up next to it. I was damn near out of the car before he had a chance to park good.

When Paul saw me he jumped out of the limo and rushed over to me.

"Sir, she is in the back. I say 'ma'am, ma'am, she's not responding!" Paul blurted out.

"Its OK Paul, I'll take care of it." I said as I continued to the limo.

"Sir, there is more." Paul said calling behind me.

I turned around to face him, waiting for him to say what he had to say.

"She ran out of the building, with no clothes on." He said in a low voice.

I had figured that Marcus would do that, which is why I called Trisha last night to bring me some clothing in Angel's size. I hoped that she wouldn't need them, but I knew Marcus to well.

"Was she hurt?" I asked.

"No sir, just afraid, and panicked." He answered sadly.

I felt a sharp zip rip through my stomach after hearing that the love of my love was afraid and while I wasn't there to protect her. I hated having to allow Angel to go through the motions with Marcus, but I couldn't do any more than she'd allow me to.

"Thank you." I said with a head nod before heading to Angel's limo.

When I opened the door I saw Angel lying on the floor with one leg in her pants as though she had been trying to get them on before she passed out.

I stepped inside the limo and felt for a pulse. When I felt that she had one and that it was strong, I was relieved. She wasn't dead, or dying, she was just passed out. So I dressed her completely, then carried her over to the Royce and lay her across the backseat.

"Paul, you have done me a service today unlike any I have ever experienced. I appreciate your time and dedication. Please, enjoy the rest of your day." I said as I counted out a thousand dollars and handed it to him.

"Why, thank you sir. It is a pleasure serving you." He said as an all knew glow took over his being. Suddenly life wasn't as gloomy for him as it had been seconds ago. Money is the best motivational speaker there ever was.

I nodded my head towards him then turned to get into my car.

When we arrived at my beach house, I paid the driver, then I carried her inside and up to a room that had one of the best views of the beach.

I had some of the older ladies in my house staff bathe and change her into a night gown, then I placed her in bed and waited for Dr. Ben to come which was about fifteen minutes later..

"She's fine, just passed out. Looks like she had a panic attack. Were you with her when it happened?" Dr. Ben asked as he jotted a few notes.

"Nah, I only found out after the fact." I said as I sat on the bed.

"Well, she'll be fine, just let her rest. If she is not awake within twenty-four hours, give me a call." He said.

"Alright, thanks for coming, this really means a lot to me." I said as I stood to my feet.

"Anytime." He said as we walked towards the door.

After showing the doctor out, I returned to Angels' room, where I opened the balcony doors to allow the fresh breeze to flow inside.

I grabbed a chair and put it next to her bed for me to sit in. Then I took her hand and closed my eyes to say a prayer within myself.

*'Father, I know she's supposed to be my wife, you have shown me that. But I need you to show me how to help her. I will never give up on her, I just need you to show me the way, in Jesus name, Amen.'*

I opened my eyes when I felt her give my hand a light squeeze, but she was still asleep. I sat back in my chair and rested my head back as I listened to the crashing waves.

\*\*\*\*

## Chapter 13

### Angel

"Angel." I heard Deytwon's voice say. I was standing in an big empty room staring out of a window that overlooked the ocean.

"Yes?" I asked turning my attention over to him.

"I have something to tell you, are you ready to hear this?" He asked as he approached me.

"Yes." I replied without thinking.

"Good, then wake up." He said.

My eyes flew open and I jumped up out of my sleep to find myself lying in a king sized bed in a  huge room. My eyes eased around the room trying to detect anything that seemed familiar enough to tell me where I was.

Everything in the room was white, from the big fluffy couches, the lounge chair, the table, the plush carpet, the the fireplace, even the curtains that danced against the breeze flying up and down. I got out of bed and walked over to the windows. That's when I noticed that I was wearing a long silk night gown.

"What the fuck?" I said aloud, wondering if I were wearing anything underneath. I felt for my bra and panties, and they were there.

"What the hell happened?" I asked myself as I continued to the window. Looking out, I saw the beach. No people, just seagulls, sand and water.

"Where am I, *Ocean City*?" I asked as I stepped onto the balcony. I welcomed the comforting feeling the warm breeze gave me as it brushed against my skin. I loved the beach, just never had the type of friends that were down to travel.

"So you're awake I see." I heard Deytwon's voice ask from behind me. Startled, I jumped then I turned around to face him.

"Deytwon." Was all that I could manage to say.

"Yes, how are you feeling?" He asked.

"I don't know, I don't even know what happened. Last thing I remember... I was dressing in the limo."I said as my heart began to sink all over again.

"Yes, then you passed out. My driver brought you to me, and I brought you here." He explained.

"But why? And how did you know that I would need your help? How did you know that I was in jail?" I asked my mouth was running a hundred miles a minute questions that I felt needed answers.

"Relax Angel. There's not much that can get passed me. I knew that you needed the limo to wait because, I know Marcus well. By me getting you out of jail, he lost respect for you, and any loyalty that he felt towards you, which trust me, wasn't much to begin with, was depleted entirely." Deytwon said.

"He was never coming to get me, was he?" I asked as I felt tears form in my eyes.

"No, he wasn't." Deytwon replied.

"But why?" I asked.

"Several reasons, soon you'll understand. Are you hungry?" Deytwon asked me.

"No, I just want to understand what's happening to me." I said feeling lost and confused.

Deytwon just looked at me and nodded his head.

"You haven't eaten in eight hours, please try to eat." He said.

"Eight hours? I've been out that long?" I asked.

"Yes, I had a doctor check in on you, he said that you were OK, but that it was best that you rest." Deytwon said.

"I would like something to drink." I touched my throat realizing that it was kind of dry.

"Come on lets go inside." He said as he touched my arm to help me.

We went and had a seat in his breakfast nook where he convinced me to eat a few bites of the food that had been prepared for me.

After that, I went and took a shower, dressed in the clothing he made available to me and rejoined him on another balcony attached to another part the the huge house. When I got there after being escorted by his maid, I saw him reclining in a lounge chair reading a book.

"Hey." I said once I stepped outside.

"Hey, how do you feel?" He asked sitting the book down on the table next to him.

"I'm alive." I replied taking a seat.

"That counts for a lot, don't you think?" He asked.

"If you say so. My life right now is very depressing, I'm back at square one." I answered ashamed of where I was as much as I was ashamed of how I got there.

"That's not a bad place to be, really when you think about it." He said.

"How you figure that?" I asked looking up at him.

"If you're at the bottom, where else can you go, but up?" He asked.

"So you're an optimist, right?" I asked standing to my feet to walk over to the railing.

"Why not? Being a pessimist doesn't solve anything." He replied,

"But being an optimist does?" I challenged.

"Well, seeing how worry causes stress, and stress causes death, I'm gonna go with yeah, it does." He answered.

"Like its really hard for you to be positive, when you have everything you could ever want at your fingertips." I said looking around at the land.

"Money and things don't equate to happiness. Its the things that you can't buy, that are worth having, that will bring you true happiness." He said.

"Yeah? Well for once I would like to be on the opposite end of that truth." I replied glancing out at the water.

"Angel, what is it that you want?" Deytwon asked after a few seconds of silence.

"To be OK" I replied.

"And what is it that you need?" He asked.

"To know that I'm OK" I answered.

"What would make you OK?" He asked walking over to me. He leaned on the railing and looked over in my direction. I returned the stare.

"I don't know." I finally replied.

He nodded his head at me then turned to look out at the water. As we stood there in silence watching the water, I began to wonder what my next game plan should be. I didn't know what Deytwon's intentions were for me, but it was time that I came up with some of my own for myself. As much of a survivor as I was, I wasn't sure if I could handle having the rug pulled from up under me again.

"You wanna take a walk?" Deytwon's voice sliced through my thoughts like a knife, but in a good way because I could feel myself getting more and more depressed.

"Deytwon, what is it that you want from me? Why am I really here" I asked ignoring his question.

"I feel compelled to protect you." He answered.

"What do you mean, protect me? And why do you feel like that's something you need to

134

do? Who are you, captain save a hoe?" I asked frustrated.

"Are you a hoe?" He asked raising an eyebrow.

"You know what I mean." I replied looking away.

"Can we sit?" He asked.

I turned and walked back over to the table to sit. He followed me over and sat across from me. He then looked at me for a few seconds before he began to speak. It was almost as if he were trying to get his words together.

"Do you keep in contact with your family at all?" He asked.

"No, I have no family." I replied with a careless shrug.

"None? No mother, grandmother, uncles, grandfather, nothing?" He asked surprised.

"*NOTHING*! My mother had me when she was fifteen, then she ran off. My grandmother raised me until she died which is when I was fourteen, and I've been on my own every since." I shot at him, I hated the story of my life.

Deytwon nodded his head before speaking again.

"Have you ever wondered about your family history?" He asked with gentle ease.

"yeah, I wondered what kind of a fucked up history would it take for a family to abandon me." I replied sarcastically.

"You've never talked about this before, have you?" He asked leaning back in his seat.

"No one's ever asked." I replied. Again he nodded his head, but this time he stretched out his hand for me to take.

"Come take a walk with me." He said,

"Where are we going?" I asked.

"Nowhere really, just on the beach for a lil while." He said.

"Why? Is that the perfect setting for you to get into my head more?" I sassed.

"Nah, I just want to get you out of your head." He replied calmly.

I shook my head at him before standing to my feet and walking back into the house. I heard him chuckle behind me.

We walked the beach talking only about how beautiful nature was, and how it was all put together to live out its course to serve a purpose and preserve itself. He didn't mention my family, my past or even my relationship with Marcus even once.

We ended up walking until the sunset, which we watched until it was completely dark. Then he called into the house to have them prepare dinner while we made our way back.

Deytwon was the perfect gentlemen, still, I wasn't yet convinced that I could trust him.

After dinner we went into his study for drinks. Every room in his home had a balcony off of it. It was like he couldn't get enough of the water, or the scenery.

He sat in a huge plush recliner that was next to a fireplace and lay his head back as though he had a long day. I sat in the recliner across from his and watched the fire burn.

"Your Brandy sir." said a maid as she entered the room.

"Thank you Rita." He said as he removed his glass from the tray.

"Your iced tea madam." The maid said as she walked over to me.

"Thank you Ms. Rita." I replied. She looked at me very strangely and smiled before nodding her head to leave.

"Why did she look at me like that?" I asked once she was out of the room.

"Because you called her Ms. She's a maid, she feels that she is to serve us, not the other way around. I used to call her Ms. until she informed me that it made her feel uncomfortable." Deytwon explained.

"Oh, OK Well, cheers." I said holding my glass up towards his. He in turn did the same then took a sip of Brandy.

"You mind if I smoke? I like to have a cigar with my Brandy." He asked as he opened a rectangular box that sat next to his recliner.

"No, I love the smell of cigars. But I don't want one, I prefer cigarettes." I said.

"Oh, I wasn't offering you one." He said as he pulled a cigar from the box.

"Wow, smack me all in the face." I replied

"No, its just that its not lady like. I will never offer you something that to me, takes away from your lady qualities." He said after lighting the cigar.

"Hence, no Brandy." I said.

"Yes, and no. A woman making power moves should sip Brandy every now and then, but not with her man." He said.

"You have all these rules of engagement for men and women in your head. But the world ain't like that anymore." I said.

"I'm not a chauvinist." He chuckled.

"I don't know." I replied shaking my head.

"I'm an idealist. What would be wrong with a World where everybody knew, and played their roll?" He asked.

"Nothing, but this world will never be like that. Too many people hating' their way to the top, or at least trying to." I answered.

"But you see, one small seed can grow into an enormous tree, one tree can start a forest." He said.

"Sorry, you lost me." I said before taking a sip.

"A man and a woman who share the same vision, same ideals, and live their lives according to standards set by these visions and ideals, and then have children born into this system, can start a movement that will never die, because it was always be in their blood to live, think and feel this way. This, can change the world" Deytwon spoke with a lot of passion.

"That's not possible, there are too many people in the world, one group of people wont inspire ten billion." I said

"Anything is possible, that's what makes the world so fascinating. The only people who believe in limits are the ones who set them for fear of knowing that there really are none." He said as he sat back in his seat.

"I see you're really into Philosophy." I said playing down my captivation of him. His passion was turning me on in a way that I had never been turned on before, and I wanted to hear more of his thoughts and beliefs.

"Philosophy, Psychology, Sociology, Anthropology,  History, Ancient Egypt, Ancient Greece, Greek Mythology, I have degrees in everything." I said after taking a pull from his cigar.

"Damn, you love school huh?" I asked.

"I love learning." He said correcting me.

"I was in college too, but that's all over now." I said as my mind slowly seeped in the thoughts of Marcus putting me out.

"What were you studying?" He asked.

"Creative writing." I replied feeling a little embarrassed as it paled in comparison to his harder courses.

"For your Poetry?" He asked. I looked up at him shocked.

"You remember me telling you that?" I asked surprised.

"I don't forget much, especially when I'm interested." He said.

"yeah, I enjoy learning about the history of Poetry, and the different schemes and things like that." I said ignoring the latter part of his statement. It gave me a fuzzy feeling and I still didn't know if I could trust him.

"That's so fuckin' cool." He said.

"Why you say that?" I asked blushing.

"Because most people don't want to take the time out to learn their craft, they just want to do it. I hate that." He said.

"So what exactly is your craft?" I asked.

"Everything." He answered smoothly.

"So you'll never stop learning." I said.

"Nope." he said

I smiled and continued to sip my tea.

(Angel)

A couple nights later, after tossing and turning my sleep away I decided to get out of bed and go sit on the balcony to watch the waves. For some reason I felt drawn to go to the one off the living room.

When I got there I saw that the doors were already open so I stepped outside and found Deytwon leaning over the railing watching the water with a glass in his hand.

"Hey." I said as I joined him at the railing.

"Hey, what you doing' up?" He asked looking over at me.

"Not a drinking problem." I said glancing down at his cup.

"This is soda." He said before taking a sip.

"Oh." I replied leaning on the railing to gaze at the water and night sky.

"And scotch." He added after his sip.

"Does drinking make you feel good?" I asked wondering if he did have a problem.

"I don't know, does not drinking make you feel good?" He asked.

"I drink, just not as much as you seem to." I said.

"Good for you." He said sitting the cup down.

"So why *do* you drink so much?" I asked.

"You've been here for how long? How did you come to this conclusion already?" He asked

"Even when I saw you at events, you always had a drink in your hand. And since I've been here, you've had at least four." I said.

"I actually don't drink as much as you think. The glass you see me with is all I have and barely ever gets refilled." He said.

"Or you can not tell me and give me a bullshit answer." I said with a chuckle.

He shook his head and let out a voiceless sigh before he spoke.

"You ever been responsible for something more powerful than yourself?" He asked still looking out at the water.

"Like a kid?" I asked.

"Jive like, but more like the King's kid." He said.

"But why would I be responsible for the king's kid?" I asked confused.

"Because it's your destiny to keep him alive and always growing and always in power." He explained.

"Dey, what are you talking about, you're not making sense." I said. He looked at me for a

Sidechick Blues The Plot by Nikida Bellezza

second then he reached for his drink.

"Yeah I am, just not right now." He said before putting his cup to his lips. I grabbed hold of the cup and took it from him then I sat it on the table, and put my arms around him.

For a few seconds he stood there not moving. Then he put his arms around me and held me tight. After a few minutes I could feel his body ease and relax. That's when I understood that he had the weight of the world on his shoulders.

*****

## Chapter 14

### Angel

The next few weeks, Deytwon and I were inseparable. We spent days enjoying nature in its natural forum as we traveled to different parts of the state, or states close by. We'd spend our evenings talking late into the night about various things. He introduced me to the appreciation of knowing and understanding why things are and how they came to be.

Not one time did he touch me, kiss me, or insinuate that he wanted to sleep with me. I was beginning to feel as though I were losing my sex appeal, but at the same time, I was starting to fall in love with him, which scared the hell out of me, because it was way too quick and my heart still needed to heal from what Marcus did to it.

The only time I really found myself thinking about Marcus, was when I realized that no man has ever made me feel the way that Deytwon made me feel. He was kind, considerate, gentle, patient, understanding and encouraging. He encouraged me to write. He encouraged me to research my subject matter and in doing so, my writing became more effective and more alive. I didn't need pain to write as I once thought, only passion, and passion had more than one source.

Today was a particularly rainy Thursday. While I sat in the study writing a poem that stretched for three pages, Deytwon sat in his recliner reading a book about the Roman Empire. Truth be told, I could feel him sneaking peeks of me from time to time, and I adored it. He always wanted to read what I wrote, and I'd always be too shy, but today would be his lucky day. This three page poem was a depiction of the way I felt about him.

"That's a long one I see." He said interrupting the quiet.

"yeah, I have a lot to say in this poem." I replied with a smile.

"Oh yeah, will this be the one that I finally get to read, or will you continue to tease me?" He asked.

"No, you can read it, but not until I'm done." I said.

"Of course." He replied with a smile.

"So what's it about?" He asked interrupting me again.

"Its about this guy, who's very impatient. He keeps interrupting the process." I answered.

"Damn, so what happens to him?" He asked playing into my sarcasm.

"He finally says, you know what, I'll wait. Then he picks his book back up and continues reading." I went on.

"Nah, I ain't got that happening, not if the guy is anything like me. You see, there's this beautiful woman who keeps teasing me with her talent. She lets me see that she has talent, but she never lets me experience it." He said.

I looked up blushing.

"That didn't come out right." He said with a chuckle.

"No, not at all." I replied laughing.

"OK, your version of the story is right, I'll wait until you have something to tell me." He said picking his book back up.

"You know what, that reminds me, that day I came here, while I was passed out, I had a dream that you said you had something to tell me." I said as the memory was triggered.

"Really? Why didn't you tell me before?" He asked surprised.

"I don't know, I guess because this whole thing is so strange." I answered with a shrug.

"I do have something to tell you, and I actually tried to before. But you didn't seem ready" he said.

"Do I seem ready now?" I asked.

"You told me about the dream, I would say you are." He replied

"Okay..." I said encouraging him to go on.

He sat his book down on the table next to him as he sat up in his seat.

"Aright, well, as you know, Marcus and I are in an Entity known as The Big Boys. But we're not only in it, we are the leaders. It was started back during slavery days by my great great grandfather, Marcus' great great grandfather and another man." Deytwon paused.

"Who was the other man?" I asked.

"*Your* great great great great-grandfather." He said after a slight pause.

"What?!" I asked shocked.

"Yes, Cecil Powers your great great grandfather is a founding father of The Big Boys. They established themselves to create a syndicate of people who wanted to help, protect and up lift others. They weren't as unfortunate as many others to be under a cruel slave master. Their slave master Norris Phillips inherited the slaves. He instead wanted to move to Paris and study, but he was forbidden by his father on his death bed, and so he took on the slaves.

There were talks, rumors of Norris wanting to set his slaves free, so during one of his journeys to trade in the cotton, he was attacked by a few sheeted men. Our great great grandfathers were always the ones to accompany Norris on his journey, and it was them who saved his life that night.

Norris was so grateful that he put in his will that the three men, our great great grandfathers were to become free men upon his death, and would also inherit his diamond and gold mines. Because he knew that they could not read, he had his Will written twice, and gave the copy to your great great grandfather who stuffed it in a trunk.

The Big Boys still operated and grew, this was during a time when black men were proud to be apart of something positive and strong. The Will was later discovered by your great grandfather who could read. He got with Marcus' and my great grand fathers and they all cashed in. It took years to get what was there's, but they got it and it's been in our blood lines every since." Deytwon explained

"Wow, this is, are you serious?" I asked trying to take it all in.

"Yes Angel, you are an extremely wealthy woman." Deytwon said.

"But, how do you know that I'm the one?" I asked feeling that it was too good to be true.

Deytwon looked at me for a few seconds, then he shook his head as if to break his train of thought.

"Marcus and I wanted to find the third heir. We did research into the bloodline and found that your great great-grandfather walked away from The Big Boys because he felt that they were heading in the wrong direction with the decisions that were being made. With all of the money backing them and all of the land they were buying up, they were growing in power. So he bowed out and kept your dad out.

The only child he had was your dad, and the only child your dad had, was you. We tracked you to your job at the MLK library. Marcus and I wanted to meet you, so we came to DC and actually spent the day at the library observing you. From the first moment I saw you, I felt that you were the most beautiful woman I had ever seen in my life. You were wearing a denim skirt..."

"With a black sweater." I said finishing his statement.

"You remember?" He asked surprised.

"yeah, that's the day I met Marcus." I answered looking away from Deytwon.

He slowly nodded his head

"I see." He replied.

"Did he know how you felt?" I asked.

"yeah, which is why he did what he did." Deytwon said as he stood to his feet. He walked over to the bar to pour himself a drink.

"I don't understand." Said.

"Marcus believes in nothing but power. How to get it, having it and how to get more. When he saw the way I felt about you he immediately decided to checkmate me." He said as he walked back over to have a seat.

"But why?" I asked clueless.

"The three of us, our bloodlines are power entities. If you and I combined, our entity together would be more powerful than his." Deytwon explained

"Power entity? Me? This sounds so wild, like I'm in the twilight zone or something." I said wondering if it could all be true. That I was really rich and had power.

"Its true, you are the only direct living heir from the Powers bloodline. You are a Queen with great power." He said.

"So, what now?" I asked as I began to feel overwhelmed, confused and more alone than I've ever been in my life.

"What you mean?" He asked.

"What do I do? Am I supposed to just go out there an live it up?" I asked.

"If you allow me, I'd like to get you acclimated to our world, before I set you loose in it." He said.

"Acclimated, like how?" I asked only half knowing what the word acclimated meant.

"I want you to study the history of the big boys. Get the principals of what it means to be a

146

leading lady. Learn etiquette, take a finance course. And you'll need to find a median, because you will definitely need one in this world of power and corruption." He said.

"What's a median?" I asked.

"Its like a belief system, something that will keep you centered and grounded." He explained.

"You mean, God?" I asked.

"yeah, do you believe in a God?" He asked.

"I believe in God." I replied.

"Do you study Him and worship?" He asked.

"No, not really." I admitted.

"Well start, because when you see how much power you hold, you are going to need an anchor, or you will become consumed and lost." Deytwon said.

"How do you stay grounded?" I asked.

"I study, because I understand that there are things that are more untouchable, more fascinating, bigger and more powerful than me. Besides that, I have a relationship with God which keeps me from going too far in any direction. This life is a muthafucka Angel, there is nothing that we can't do. Leaders come to us for various things. We control so much and its very overwhelming, because we are so young. But we have a position to up hold, a position that has been passed down through our bloodline, and we have the responsibility to honor it, protect it and keep it alive." He said.

"What if I can't live up to it? What if I fail?" I asked nervously.

"That's why if you believe in God, you gotta get your weight up in faith." He said.

"I don't know Dey, this seems like too much. I don't think I'm ready." I said wondering if

I really wanted parts of this life that he was describing.

"You're not, but I won't leave your side until you are." He said.

I found comfort in his words, but at the same time, disappointment. I was happy to know that he would have my back, but I didn't want his role in my life to decrease. Deytwon was unlike any man that I had ever met. I really enjoyed his company in a different way, in that, I always found myself learning something new, or being intrigued to want to learn more about any given subject.

He showed me things that I would've never seen for myself. Even though I wasn't an ugly chick, he made me feel more beautiful and special. He made me feel like a lady, and I have never had a man make me feel these things or want better for myself.

"You OK?" He asked interrupting my thoughts.

"yeah, why?" I asked.

"You just got real quiet on me, and started looking out into the distance." He said with a chuckle.

"Nah, yeah, I just had something on my mind." I replied.

"Wanna talk about it?" He asked.

"Nah, I'm good." I said.

"Cool, so we start your training on Monday?" He asked.

"That works, I guess." I replied.

"Angel." He said.

"yeah?" I asked looking up at him.

"As long as you need me, I will be there." He assured me.

My heart smiled, and so did I.

## Chapter 15

### Angel

That Monday, Deytwon flew in an etiquette specialist from England who discussed proper manners and the behaviors of a Lady to no end. Between her accent and me making the same mistakes over and over again I wanted to jump out the window screaming "*Fuck it!*" But nevertheless she was very patient and kind. The hardest part of the lessons were letting go of the 'Street jive' talk, as she so eloquently put it, and use proper English. *'Pardon me, but fuck you, madam!'* is what I wanted to say.

Two hours after that the Big Boy representative came to discuss the history of the organization with me. He had books and everything. It was pretty interesting how they got their start, how they grew and what their creed is. A lot of it was what Deytwon had already told me, but this guy went into more depth with it.

Two days later Deytwon flew in some hot shot from Wall Street to discuss the art of finance with me. His lessons were actually interesting. He had a strong passion for money, getting it and making it grow. I enjoyed his discussion.

But my favorite session was with the dance teacher that he flew in from South America. He was very handsome, but pretty at the same time, and he could move in ways that made you think he had no bones in his body. He was teaching me how to do some kind of sultry salsa dance, but I wasn't getting it. I was too used to dancing to Gogo and R&B music. It seemed to take me forever to get the dance moves right, but by three weeks in, I could move with the best of them.

One afternoon during the dance session Deytwon sat in and watched. I was nervous as hell, but I was happy to show him that the lessons were paying off.

149

Sidechick Blues The Plot by Nikida Bellezza

As the dance teacher twirled me around, dipping me, pulling me, guiding me here and there I couldn't help but to notice Deytwon's eyes watching intensively.

"Focus!" The teacher demanded with a slap to my ass. I returned my eyes to him and continued to dance in tune with his lead.

For the first time this type of dance felt natural. My body took to the movements as though it were specifically built to move this way. I didn't count the steps, I didn't wonder how I looked nor did I feel embarrassed about what I was doing, because I finally understood that if it felt this good, it had to look damn good.

At the end Ricardo bent me into a slow deep dip, and pulled me out of it all in the same movement. I looked over at Deytwon whose eyes were locked in on me. He said nothing, nor did he move. Ricardo laughed as he leaned into me.

"I know that look, somebody gonna get it tonight. He's gorgeous, you go mami!" He whispered before walking off.

"So?" I asked as Deytwon walked over to me.

"That was perfect." He said.

"Thank you." I replied blushing all over myself.

"You hungry?" He asked.

"yeah, a little." I said.

"Cool, why don't you go change." He said.

"Into what, where are we going?" I asked.

"Anything you want, it will only be the two of us." He answered.

"OK" I replied before leaving the room.

I went up to my room and showered, then I went inside my closet to find something to

150

wear. I chose a pink v-neck t-shirt and a jean skirt. He loved me in pink and I didn't want to waste an outfit if we weren't really going anywhere.

When I got downstairs he was waiting by the door wearing a polo shirt and some jeans. He noticed me and smiled before he opened the door.

"You ready?" he asked holding his arm out for me to take.

"Yes sir." I replied.

We stepped outside to see a horse and carriage waiting in front of the house.

"Oh my." I said as I brought my hand up to my mouth.

The driver stepped out and opened the little door for us and Deytwon helped me up into the carriage.

"I *so* did not expect this!" I said never in a million years thinking I'd be the girl to experience this.

"Just a lil something." He said as he took his seat next to me.

I wrapped my arm around his and enjoyed the view as the carriage carried us along the beach.

"The water is so mesmerizing at night, I love it." I said looking out across the ocean.

"I know, you say that every time." he replied.

"Oh." I said feeling a little embarrassed.

"Close your eyes." He said after we had been riding for a bit.

"OK" I said complying.

Soon the carriage stopped and I heard the door open for us to exit.

"Keep them closed and take my hand." He said as I felt his hand on mine.

I stood up and allowed him to guide me out of the carriage. Then I felt the strangest thing,

I was being swooped up into his arms and I couldn't believe it. Sure I've been carried by a man before, but it was usually over to a bed, never as an innocent sweet gesture.

"What's going on?" I asked with a giggle, which was strange, where did this girly side of me come from!

"Open you eyes." He said once he stopped walking.

I opened my eyes to see a table set with candles surrounded by 4 tiki posts across from a beautifully arranged buffet.

"Oh my gawd!" I said as Deytwon stood me up next to him.

"Thanks sir, see you in about two hours, unless it rains, then come immediately." Deytwon said as he turned and shook hands with the man driving the carriage.

"Thank you, sir." The man replied.

"Deytwon, this is so beautiful, but why?" I asked ready to shed girly tears.

"Why not?" He asked as he pulled my seat out for me.

I sat down and watched him walk over to take his seat.

"You have been so kind to me. I can't say that I deserved it, but no man has been the way you are with me." I said.

"I believe that we are meant to have certain experiences, to teach us to appreciate other experiences." He said.

"That makes sense." I said nodding my head.

"Good evening, madam, sir. Are you ready to eat at this time?" Asked a man in a waiters uniform.

"Are you?" Deytwon asked me.

"Yes, please." I replied putting my etiquette training to work.

"Yes, we're ready." Deytwon said to the waiter.

Our food was brought over to us just as I heard a soft violin start to play. I looked over in the corner and saw a small band sitting behind the tiki posts.

"You thought of everything." I said with a huge smile.

"But you make it all come together." He replied causing me to blush.

"Thank you." I said bashfully.

"So how are your sessions coming along?" He asked. I supposed to break the rising tension.

"Wonderfully, well, at first I found them kind of boring. Then the information started growing on me and grabbed my interest. They kind of make me miss college." I said.

"Then go to College. These sessions aren't a substitute for college, they're more like a crash course." He said.

"Well, I haven't been to class in months, I'm sure they withdrew me." I said thinking about my classes at UDC.

"I'm confident that they did, but you can always do online schooling." He said.

"yeah, but, I prefer to be in a classroom, I like that group, teacher in the front, ask questions get the answers now, type setting." I said.

"I feel you on that, the only thing is, you have a coronation coming up in seven months." He said.

"Coronation?" I asked.

"Its a ceremony where we will present you with a Big Boy ring, and crown you as Queen. Marcus and I are the Kings. This is a very big deal because you will complete the trio, and this will be the first time in 50 years that we've had the third member in position. On top of that, you

153

are the first Queen that we have ever had." He said.

"What about the wives of the Big Boys?" I asked.

"They become first lady's, only the daughter of a King who has no son's can become a Queen, other wise, you'd be more like a princess, which is still much higher than the wives." He explained.

"Were you ever married?" I asked.

"Nope, never." He replied.

"Why not, don't you ever want to get married?" I asked.

"When the time is right." He answered.

"How will you know when that is?" I inquired.

"She'll make me feel a way that no other woman has ever made me feel. And when I look in her eyes, I'll see my future." He said.

"That's going to be special. I hope that someone will love me like that one day. A man who doesn't belong to anyone else, but me." I said.

"It will happen for you, don't worry about it, just live, when the time is right, you'll know." He said. I nodded my head feeling a little disappointed that he didn't even seem to be considering me.

I was really falling for Deytwon hard. I never felt this way about a man before. I loved who I was and who I was becoming when I was with him. He showed me that I can do better, and that I should always dig deeper in this thing called life. For the first time in my life, I believed that sky was the limit.

After dinner we walked along the beach for a bit, then we returned to the horse and carriage and rode back to the house. It was a perfect evening, and even though it was late, I didn't want it to end.

Deytwon walked me to my room, he had to go handle some business early in the morning so he wanted to turn in for the night. On our trek to my room I couldn't help but feel a little nervous, wondering if this were going to be *the night.* I wanted to experience him sexually, but I enjoyed the waiting game. I felt respected, appreciated and interesting.

"Well, here we are." He said when we got to my door.

"Yes, here we are." I replied bashfully, though I couldn't figure out why, it ain't like I never had sex before.

"I had a good time tonight, as always, I enjoyed your company." He said.

"So did I. It was a beautiful evening, very romantic." I said.

"That was the plan, simple and sweet." He replied.

"Yeah, it worked well." I added.

"Well, aright Angel, good night my lady." He said as he kissed my hand.

"Good night, Dey." I replied dryly before turning to go inside my room. I was a little sadden, not because we didn't have sex, but because he wasn't more affectionate with me, and I wasn't even sure if he wanted to be.

"Whoa, what was that?" He asked turning me back around to face him.

"Nothing, I'm good." I lied.

"Nah, you beefin' about something, you wanna tell me about it?" He asked.

I shook my head and looked away from him.

"Be a woman about yours. You're about to become a Socialite, a Queen over a very powerful organization, speak with boldness, own up to what you feel." He said.

"Dey, I've never met a man like you." I began

155

"Because that's impossible, but go on." He said.

"I mean, you don't feel anything... for me? I mean, you don't hug me, you don't kiss me, you don't take my hand." I said not looking at him.

He raised my chin so that our eyes would meet.

"I don't do those things, because they are too forward for what I'm trying to accomplish with you." He said.

"What does that mean?" I asked shaking my head.

"It means, that I'm old fashion, I like to court first. Get to know you, you get to know me, we feel each other out." He said.

"I understand that but, I don't turn you on? I mean, you never try to kiss me or be affectionate with me." I said.

"I'm on fire for you Angel, I just can't do nothing about it, I'm bound." He said.

"Bound by what?" I asked confused.

"An agreement I made with God. When I was a lil younger, I used to be untamed. I was heavily into partying, drinking, smoking, and doing' whatever. I vowed to have sex with at least one woman from every continent, and I did, well, except for Antarctica of course. I felt invincible and I lived like I was. You see, when you have total power, if you're not guided properly, you'll become susceptible to it. The saying is true, absolute power corrupts absolutely." He explained.

"OK, but like, when did you learn your lesson?" I asked wanting him to finish the story of his life.

"Aright, so I had a collection of motorcycles that I used strictly for racing. I guess I thought I was Evel Knievel or something. I took all challenges, performed all stunts, and made millions in bets. So one day I decided to jump from one building to another. Simple stunt, I'd

156

done several times before, no big deal. But with these buildings, my cockiness had me underestimating how far apart they were, and I crashed through the window of the other building. I was rushed to the hospital and they didn't think I was going to make it. I was in a coma, but I could hear what they were saying. So I prayed, I told God that if he lets me live, I'll change my lifestyle and stop living like I had a death wish. From there I grew up, and let all that bad boy stuff go. I mean, I still ride every now and then, but I don't race anymore." He said.

"I see." I replied still wondering why he wouldn't touch me.

"Angel, I've been having meaningless sex, all my life. I've done everything sexually that I've ever wanted to do, except, make love, because I've never been in love with anyone in my entire life, so far. I don't want just sex anymore, I don't want a fuck buddy, I want more." He said.

"I can relate." I replied looking down at my fingers.

We stood there in silence for a few seconds listening to each other breathe, until I felt him lift my chin again.

I looked up into his eyes about as deeply as he was looking into my own, right up until he moved in to softly kiss my lips. The kiss was so tender and sweet that it sent chills all through my body, and gave me butterflies in my stomach. It was so intense that I had to pull away. His kiss had me feeling things that I had never felt before. It was like the kind of kiss women on TV say exist, but you never think you'd experience in a million years.

"Good night, Angel." He said.

"Good night." I replied still in a daze. I turned and went into my room. After I undressed and put on my night gown, I lie in bed and thought of Deytwon until I fell asleep.

The next day I showered and dressed, then I headed downstairs for brunch as it was mid morning.

      As I walked passed the study I peeked in to see Deytwon standing next to my chair reading something.

      "Good morning." I said tapping on the wall.

      He turned around and looked at me with a slightly confused expression on his face.

      "What?" I asked.

      "You're in love with me?" He asked.

      That's when I looked down and noticed that he was holding my 3 page poem in his hand.

      "Oh my gawd, you're reading that?" I asked surprised and embarrassed.

      "One, You didn't answer my question, and two, you said that I could." He replied.

      "Yes, I said you could when I was finished, I wasn't finished!" I exclaimed trying to take the papers from his hand.

      "But it said *"The End"* at the bottom, what were you going to write next, an epilogue?" He asked swinging the papers out of my reach.

      "Please give them to me." I begged.

      "I already finished reading it." He said.

      I shook my head before turning to walk away.

      "You still never answered my question." He said calling behind me.

      I turned back around to face him but I didn't speak.

      "Are you falling in love with me, is that what this poem is about?" He asked as he walked closer to me.

      "The poem is about a woman, who feels something for a man that she has never felt before. She believes that its love, and she wants it to be reciprocated" I explained trying to play it

158

down.

"And who's the woman?" He asked.

I looked at Deytwon hard, watching him standing there waiting for his question to be answered. I had never been put on the spot like this before, and it felt strange being made to feel this vulnerable. It was scary to have all of your cards on the table and not knowing exactly what the other person was capable of doing with them.

"Me." I finally admitted with a shrug.

"And who is the man?" He asked.

"*You*." I replied after a deep sigh.

"So then this poem, is what you feel." He asked.

"Yes." I replied.

"Would you like to know how I feel?" He asked .

I looked up at him and nodded my head as my heart began to pound fast and heavy.

"The exact same way." He said.

I could feel myself blushing as he walked over to me and took me into his arms. I held him back as tight as I could. I needed to be sure that this was real and not a dream. Have I finally found the type of love that always seemed to escape me? Have I finally found someone that was ready to be all about me, and that I didn't have to share, and that wouldn't sacrifice my heart to follow their own dreams. Did I finally matter to someone? These thoughts brought tears to my eyes and I begin to cry.

Deytwon let me go and looked down at me, to see my tears.

"I'm sorry." I said for a lack of excuse for my tears.

"Trust me, I get it, and it will be OK I promise, they will always only be happy, until the

159

day I die." He said.,

I threw my arms around him and just held on to him, never wanting to let go.

*****

## Chapter 16

### Marcus

This was probably the best cigar I had ever had, or at least had in a long time. The pull was easy, the aroma was intoxicating. It filled the entire room, overpowering all other scents in the air. I loved that shit, any type of power was my type of shit.

I had been sitting in a leather barker lounger facing a bay window that over looked the big city lights. I loved windows with views showing me a world that was mine. Much of what I could see was either properties that I owned or properties that I could purchase. Either way, it was all candy land to me.

My guest of honor arrived like clockwork, right on time.

"Trisha, glad you could make it." I said after opening the door to let her in.

"Tardiness is bad for business." She replied cheerfully.

"That it is." I said with a smile and a wink.

"So who is the lucky new lady that I get to decorate?" She asked following me further into the apartment.

"Oh, no project like that today. I want you to sit and chat with me a lil bit. You mind?" I asked stretching my arm out towards the couch.

"Oh, OK Is something wrong?" She asked a bit hesitant.

"Nah, just want you to watch some old home movies with me." I said as I took up the remote control to turn on the 50" television.

"Do me a favor, pick up the remote in front of you and hit play." I said.

"OK" She said reaching for the remote.

I watched her manicured finger gently press the play button as her eyes eagerly watched the screen.

*"....Then what makes them untouchable.."*

*"Power, their money is powerful across the globe.."*

*"What the fuck, if they had that kinda bread, why do they live in the dmv.."*

"Marcus, what is this?" Trisha asked after a few seconds of viewing the video.

"You tell me, or better yet, tell me more about this." I said fast forwarding the video a little more.

*"....it's said that there were three men but no one knows what happened to the third one. But the three started the Big Boys Organization back when they were slaves..."* I paused the video and looked over at Trisha whose mouth and eyes were wide open.

"Marcus, you watched this, so you saw that she kept badgering me! What was I to do?" Trisha asked in a panic.

"Not what you *did*." I replied with a chuckle.

"I didn't tell her everything. I didn't, I swear to god! You watched the tape, you know I didn't tell her what I accidentally found out." Trisha said as she jumped to her feet. I smiled and took a pull from my cigar.

"What did you find out?" I asked with a smile. I already knew but I wanted to see if she were dumb enough to repeat it After I forced her to take a blood oath not to.

"That, Cecil Powers Jr, was really assassinated." She stuttered.

"Good girl. Hey, you're shivering, would you like some Cocoa?" I asked.

"Yes, please." She accepted.

"I'll get it for you." I said with a smile before heading towards the front door.

I walked pass my assassin Cocoa Killer and winked before leaving the condo.

Meanwhile at the same time in another part of town...

### Deytwon

"My son." My father said once his face appeared on the screen. I called him for a little video chat. He and my mom had taken up residence in Italy a few years ago, so from time to time we video chat to keep in touch.

"Pop, how's it going, how's mom?" I asked.

"All's well, all's well. So how are you liking life back in the States? He asked.

"Its cool, I plan to settle down here which is why I called." I said.

"You don't mean... " My father started.

"Yes pop, I met her. I met my wife to be." I said trying to suppress the smile that fought to conquer my face.

"So it seems you have. So what's the problem?" He asked.

"You tell me. She's the new heiress" I said now more seriously.

"Oh, I see." My father said.

"So does that make her off limits to me? Am I violating sanctions here or what?" I asked ready for him to give it to me straight.

"Well let me ask you this son, would it matter to you If you were?" He asked.

I looked up at my dad and shook my head.

"No." I answered confidently.

"Then marry her." He said

"Just like that, I have your blessing?" I asked as I felt a weight lift off me.

"Not that you needed it, but yes." He said.

"Thanks man, that means a lot to me." I said wishing that I could hug him

"Have you asked her yet?" He asked.

"No, I'm going to ask her Friday night." I replied thinking about our big date.

"Nervous?" He asked with a chuckle.

"Out my mind, but I know this is right. I knew it the moment I saw her for the first time." I explained.

"Then a long engagement would be pointless. Have a midnight ceremony after the coronation." My dad suggested.

"*Seriously*?" I asked.

"Go for it." He said

"Aright, I will." I said nodding my head happy that everything seemed to be working out perfectly.

****

## Chapter 17

### Angel

"So have you decided where you want to go on our date?" Deytwon asked as he rubbed my feet. We had been lying on the day bed in his movie room watching movies all morning. After working hard for a month straight, we decided that we needed a chill day. We still hadn't gone all the way sexually, but I was in no rush, it was enough to just be in his arms.

"Uhm, I don't know, why don't you just surprise me." I said.

"I can do that, so Friday, that's cool right, you don't have any sessions on Friday do you?" He asked.

"No, not a one." I replied.

"Bet, I got some business to take care of in the morning, but I'll be back home around seven, we can leave at eight, cool?" He asked.

"Icy." I replied with a chuckle as I crawled down to where he was and lay up against him. He put his arms around me and we continued to watch the movie until the movie was watching us.

Deytwon kept whatever plans he had for us for Friday a total secret. So in order to keep from allowing anticipation to get the better of me, I spent the next four days keeping busy.

I wrote poetry, I studied the information that was provided to me by my instructors, and at night, we took walks along the beach talking about any and everything, but most times, nothing at all.

These things made the week fly by, and when Friday finally rolled around I was ready. I got a new dress and shoes, and made an appointment with my girl Karen do get my hair done.

165

I hadn't been back on the South side in so long, it looked different to me, and it seemed a lot smaller.

"BITCH! Where in the fuck you been?" Karen exclaimed as I walked through the doors of her salon.

"What the hell? Hello to you to miss." I said with a chuckle, it was interesting how not being in the hood for several months could make you feel so out of place when you got back.

"Nah, uh uh, where you been? Even Salisha said she ain't been seeing' you, she said you quit your job and every thing, now what's going on?" Karen demanded.

"Girl, I've been in school, I've been really busy because I'm trying to finish." I said only half telling the truth. The last thing I needed was the streets talking about me.

"You in *school*? Studying what? And why the fuck you talking' like a white girl?" She asked folding her arms.

"Studying literature, and why I have to be talking like a white girl because I'm not using slang?" I asked.

"Because you is, and you ain't got no job, but you can afford to go to school?" Where they do that at? And, uh uh, bitch, did you just pull up in a fuckin' Benz?" Karen asked glancing out of the window.

"I know what it is, shawty got some money dick!" Tasha exclaimed as they slapped hands

"That's what it sounds like to me!" Karen said as she started laughing.

"Anyway, you going' do my hair or what?" I asked.

"Man I'm just messing' wit' you. I got you, come on let me wash you up. I got to catch you up on this bullshit that's been happening around here anyway." Karen said

Once my hair was done I paid and tipped Karen then I decided to head over to Salisha's house. It had been many months since I've seen her and Steve. I did miss them dearly, they were the only people in my life that were like family.

When I pulled up to the complex I parked the car and walked inside the building. I knocked on Salisha's door twice before she opened it.

"Get the fuck outta here!" She asked before pulling me into a hug.

"Girlah!" I exclaimed happy to see her to but needing her to be careful not to mess up my hair.

"Girl, what is going on with you?!" Salisha exclaimed once we let go.

"Girl, so much has happened, I wouldn't even know where to begin telling you. But anyway, hows everything going? Hows Anthony?" I asked as I sat next to her on the couch.

"Oh, we good, he good. He just got a job with the Post office so we talking about getting a lil townhouse within the next few months." She said excited.

"Oh OK, that sounds good." I said happy for her

"Well, you're looking good, you still with Marcus?" She asked.

"Nah, we had a falling out, its over for good now." I said not wanting to give too much details about how Marcus carried me. Even though I was over it, I didn't want to hear the big '*I told you so*'

"Oh OK, so where you staying' now?" She asked.

"I have a place, I'm good, I started going to school, studying literature." I said.

"Ohhhh, that's what's up. I'm so glad you're doing something positive with yourself. I was so worried about you." She said.

"yeah, I know, and I'm sorry, but believe me, I'm good, we all have to go through something before we can go on to something better." I said.

"Well look at you, miss educated. Girl you are so not the same, and I mean that in a good way." She said.

"Thank you, I feel different, I feel better, and I'm happy." I replied.

"That's all I wanted to hear." Salisha said touching my hand.

Salisha and I talked for a couple hours, then I left out. I didn't want to be late for my date with Deytwon and seeing how he lived about an hour away, I figured I'd better get a move on. I asked Salisha to tell Steve that I said hello, and then I was on my way.

When I finally got back to Deytwon's house it was just after five o'clock, so I chilled on the couch and watched a movie.

About an hour later I heard movement coming towards me, thinking that it was Deytwon attempting to run up and scare me, I turned around to surprise him, but instead I saw Marcus.

"What are you doing here?!" I asked shocked to shit.

"Bitch please, thought you might have wanted to see something." He said as he dropped a picture on the table in front of me. I looked down at the picture and immediately got sick...

### Deytwon

As I sat in the thick of traffic I rest my head back on my head rest and allowed Angel's being to form in my mind. I felt a smile stretch across my lips, as I reveled in the thoughts, the knowledge that this woman was finally mine. It used to kill me to see her with Marcus, knowing that he was dogging her out. Using her ignorance as momentum to ruin her to keep her from discovering her dynasty, all to keep her away from me. That nigga had the nerve, the gall to challenge me.

I had to chuckle to myself at that one. In all the years he's known me, he didn't know me. But that's how it should be, never let the left hand know what the right hand is doing.

If I were a pettier man I could've just ordered his demise. The moves he was pulling on Angel, the heiress were strictly forbidden. Lucky for him, I'm only a petty man, and his lesson was coming like a thief in the night.

I shook my head as I pressed my foot on the gas to keep a steady flow with the traffic. If I wanted to I could charter a helicopter to get me out of this mess and just have my car shipped, but I didn't want to close down the highway. It really wasn't that serious, besides, my thoughts of Angel had me feeling like I was somewhere chilling' rather than in the heart of heavy traffic.

I had just returned from New York where I bought her diamond engagement ring. When I walked in, everyone looked at me as though I were some crazy nigga who slipped by security.

But when they saw the Big Boy Ring they shut down the store. Brought in a lounge chair, offered me a cigar and a drink and brought me their best collection of rings.

When I was younger that shit used to trip me out, to see people treating my dad like a god, and now me. Of course it's nothing to me now, but still, I won't settle for less.

When I made it back to my beach house I noticed car tracks that I didn't recognize leading from the main road down into my property. So I activated my bullet proof shield around my car and turned to head towards the downgrade behind my house.

My heart pumped thinking that something could have  happened to Angel but I didn't want to call her to check. I wanted to walk in on it whatever it was, seeing how there were no tracks leading away from my place, I knew the perp was still there.

When I got to the bottom of the downgrade, I placed my palm against a cement rock and the wall opened. I drove through and watched the door slide close behind me in my rear view mirror.

From there I hoped out of my car and punched at my wall which was made to crack like glass to reveal safe. After scanning my eye the safe opened and I reached in to grab my smith and Wesson .500 magnum.

Once I confirmed that it was loaded, I tucked it and took a passageway that lead through the walls in my house. I started hearing voices as I got closer to my living room. It was Angel and Marcus.

"What the fuck?" I said as I listened in..

### Angel

"Oh my gawd!" I screamed through a voice that I didn't even know I had.

It was a pic of Trisha sprawled on the floor with her neck wide open.

"What, what's wrong?" Marcus asked as though he were confused.

"Why?" I asked as tears ran a marathon through my eyes.

"So I got to watching the tapes of the activities that happened at the condo, and I came to realize that this bitch talked too much, so I thought she could use another mouth, only she didn't survive the operation." He said as he sat next to me.

"What do you want Marcus?" I asked scared of what he might do to me.

"You, gone... and we can do this two ways. But I'll let you decide first." He said.

"Why?" I asked.

"Cause you a dirty bitch and you don't belong in our world. You fuck me, then you fuck the other boss. Who does that? Besides, what he give you that I couldn't?" He asked

"Love." I replied.

"Love? Bitch did you just say love though? What the fuck is that?" Marcus asked with a sick laugh.

"Its everything you never had, and everything you ever wanted." I said

"Think so?" He asked with a chuckle.

"Everybody wants love, Marcus." I said.

"See, that shit right there is why you'll always be a anything, nothing ass bottom feeder. The people on the bottom want love. Us folks on the top, know that it's all about money. Money can buy anything, love will just get you another dumb muthafucka to stare at." He said before dropping an envelope and a ticket on the table next to the picture.

"What's this?" I asked.

"Your second choice. You can take this two mil and this plane ticket and get ghost, but you can't ever come back. Or, you can stay and become a ghost like your homegirl." He explained.

"So I'm just supposed to disappear without a trace?" I asked.

Marcus smiled and tapped his nose.

"Paris is very nice this time of year." He replied.

"But Deytwon will think I've abandoned him." I said shaking my head.

"What's worse, you abandoning him, or your soul abandoning your body?" Marcus asked seriously.

"OK, I'll go." I said as more tears gathered. I knew that Marcus was capable of doing whatever he said he would do. I regretted the day that I met him and the day I allowed myself to be a pawn in his plot against me.

"Good, don't worry about gathering your shit, just get in the car and roll the fuck out. Your flight leaves in two hours from Reagan, you'll be wanting to get a move on it now." He said as he stood to his feet.

"OK" I replied full of anger hurt and hatred. I supposed that karma really wasn't done with me. I did the crime and was paying for it by sacrificing my chance to be happy. I didn't care about not being able to be wealthy, I mean, that did blow me, but you can't miss what you've never had. My true sacrifice was not being able to be with the only man that I knew without question, loved me, and that I loved.

Marcus gave me that same evil smile he did the day he put me out of his condo ass naked, before leaving the room. A few seconds later I heard the door open and close, and then a car taking off.

"I am so sorry Dey, this is all my fault, had I never gotten involved with him, none of this would've happened. I love you so much, I hope you understand that." I said aloud feeling as though his heart would hear me.

Then I reached down to grab the plane ticket and walked out of the room and towards the door. Before I got to the door I felt myself being grabbed. That's when I looked up to see Deytwon.

"Dey?!" I exclaimed throwing my arms around him.

Deytwon put a finger to his lips to hush me, then he pulled out some kind of remote control.

"Look outside." He said in a low voice just as he pushed a button on the remote control.

I turned towards the window and looked around until I noticed the Benz that he was letting me drive start up and move.

"But how did.." I started but Deytwon quieted me.

"Shhh, just watch." He said as the car began to pick up speed. It sped down to the end of the driveway and almost out of sight just before it exploded.

"OH MY GAWD!" I shouted as my legs got weak.

"He, he was going to kill me?!" I said barely getting the words out as Deytwon caught me before I hit the floor.

He lift me up into his arms and carried me over to the couch where he sat me down. Then he reached for the envelope and tore it open to reveal that it was only shredded paper tightly packed inside. I shook my head as the tears started to flood my eyes.

"I almost died." I cried nearly choking on my sobs.

Deytwon reclined the couch and pulled me over to lay on him as he held me in his arms.

Feeling extremely vulnerable and afraid, I held onto him and hid from the world in his arms where he allowed me to cry myself to sleep.

**Marcus**

Through my rear view mirror I watched as pieces of the Benz joined the smoke in the air. The impact from the explosion gave my car a little jolt, but that was nothing compared to the exhilaration that I was feeling knowing that that bitch was now dead. Finally the job was done and she was no longer a threat to my riches.

If Deytwon knew her level of threat to us, he'd probably be relieved to, whether his love for her was true or not. The fact still remained the bitch's bloodline had lordship over ours, and I wasn't rocking'. Fuck that, I loved being in charge, I loved being on top answering to no one, and I wasn't about to give that up, especially not to no bitch.

Truth be told, Deytwon couldn't really be mad, had he minded his business while I was talking to the detective, he never would've known about her in the first place. But nah, nigga, you had to ear hustle and then want in on this shit. Then too, I guess I could've met up with the detective *after* my Father's birthday celebration, that way no one would've known that I had intended on finding the heir. Either way, it didn't fuckin' matter now, the bitch was dead and out of the way.

I turned on the radio and started bobbing my head to the song 'Money Power Respect' that just so happened to be playing as if on cue.

\*\*\*\*

## Chapter 18

### Angel

Later that night, hours after settling in Deytwon's bedroom, we lay in his bed staring at the ceiling, listening to the waves crash against the shore on this particularly windy night.

So much was on my mind that I found myself easily lost within my thoughts. The only thing that brought me back to reality was noticing the changes in his heartbeat every now and then. For a time our hearts would beat at the same pace, then after a while, his would change, or maybe it was mine that changed with my thoughts.

"Angel." I heard him say as my name vibrated through his chest.

"Yes?" I asked.

"Why didn't you take the envelope, when you thought that there was money inside?" He asked.

"I don't know, I guess because I felt like, nothing' in my life would ever matter again after losing you." I admitted.

"So you were going to go to Paris, flat broke?" He asked.

"I've lived broke all my life, whats the difference?" I asked back.

"Its another country, you might be able to survive here, but you don't know the ways of people in Paris, their laws, their hoods." He said.

"Does it matter, I would've never made it off your property, remember, the car exploded." I said as I sat up in bed.

"My bad, baby, I just never had anybody choose me over money before, especially in situations where they thought they lost me, and still didn't take the money." He explained.

176

"No woman has ever loved you before?" I asked.

"To be honest Angel, I don't know, and I never cared, because I never loved them, never even considered being in love. Not until I got older, but I stopped dating and looking a long time ago, because no one grabbed my attention, and if a woman couldn't grab my attention, I felt dating her would be a waste of time." He said.

"Marcus told me that you used to date his wife, but she left you for him and you haven't dated since." I said.

"That nigga, I swear, he makes it real hard to abide by the bylaws sometimes." Deytwon said sounding annoyed.

"What you mean?" I asked.

"Well, for instance, if you were a full fledged Big Boy, he would have to be killed for what he tried to do to you. He can do anything he wants to anybody else, but not to a leader, or an elder. That's why its important to have this coronation for you, because once you're crowned, he can no longer touch you." Deytwon said.

"How did he become so cruel though?" I asked.

"His love of power. But in his defense, he wasn't always like this. I've known Marcus my whole life, when our fathers were in power they grew us up together to keep us close, because we were next in line. He used to be a real cool dude. He started organizations that help the less fortunate, single mothers, low income families, across the US.

He's started charities and he still gives to many charities. Just, one day, after our coronation, his eyes flashed red, and have been that way every since." Deytwon explained.

"So *did* you date his wife?" I asked bringing the conversation back around because I really did want to know.

"Nah, but I did meet her first. Her dad is an oil tycoon, one of the few black men that owned his oil rig. He used to try to get us to date. She's very beautiful and smart, and funny, but she did nothing for me. I introduced her to Marcus, and she instantly fell in love, I believe he did too. It wasn't until the first time I saw you that I understood what they experienced. " Deytwon said.

"You fell in love with me the first time you saw me?" I asked.

"Yes ma'am. I knew nothing about you, only that I had to have you. Not thinking about what it would mean to us, I told Marcus and next thing I know, you're at my Side Chick restaurant opening." He said with a chuckle.

"Yeah, so you still running that?" I asked with a laugh.

"Oh yeah, business is booming. I opened three more out here and two in New York. I'm about to light the East Coast up. The idea is, to make her feel special by taking her to a nice classy place, that's designed specifically for side chicks. If niggas can keep their mouths closed, the chick will think she's winning." He said.

"I still think that's messed up." I replied shaking my head.

"Maybe so, but its a money maker." He said.

"yeah yeah, next subject please." I said.

"Whats on your mind?" He asked with a laugh.

"Where were we going to go on our date tonight?" I asked.

"Well, do you want me to tell you, or would you rather find out?" He asked.

"Find out when?" I asked.

"Now." He said.

"But its like two in the morning." I replied.

"Don't give me an excuse, just say yes or no." He said.

"OK, yes." I said.

"Bet, let me go make a phone call, go hop in the shower." He said as he got out of bed.

"What should I wear?" I asked.

"Anything, its late!" He said before leaving the room.

I got out of bed and went into my room where I showered and changed into some jeans and a sweater, then I met Deytwon downstairs. He was still talking on the phone.

"yeah, gassing' up right now, then we'll be on the way." I heard him say.

"Ready?" I asked.

"Yes, just as I've said, thanks man for working this out for me on short notice. OK, be there shortly." Deytwon said before ending the call.

"Yup, lets be out." He holding his arm out for me to take. I linked arms with him and we walked out of the door.

We got into the limo that was waiting out front and rode around to the back of the house where there was a jet waiting for us.

"We're flying?" I asked surprised as we stepped out of the limo.

"Yes, are you scared to fly?" He asked as he took my hand.

"No, I'm just thinking that its got to be three am." I said.

"Time stops for no man, especially not one with money." He said as we walked over to the jet.

We boarded the six-cheater taking seats facing one of another. It was very cozy and resembled a log cabin on the inside.

"Comfy?" He asked as his phone rang.

"Very." I replied.

"Cool, buckle up. We're about to take off... Jo, tell me something good." Deytwon said to me before answering his phone.

As the jet took off I looked out of the window and watched us raise from the ground into the air. I watched the house get smaller and smaller until It was completely out of sight. That's when I turned my sights to the ocean.

"Hors d'oeuvre for the lady?" A flight attendant asked offering me a plate of finger foods.

"Yes, thank you." I said taking a napkin and grabbing what I wanted.

"Would the lady like a drink?" He asked.

"Coke if you have it." I replied thinking it'd be a good idea to stay awake for this midnight date.

"That's whats up, thanks man, you stay coming' through for a brother. I will not forget this." I heard Deytwon say as he turned down the Hors d'oeuvre.

"Good news I presume?" I asked jokingly as he got off of the phone.

"The best news. But on another note, we won't going back to that beach house, we'll be going to my house in Roanoke." He said.

"Out VA?" I asked.

"yeah, I can't risk him knowing that you're alive before your coronation. Speaking of which, starting tomorrow, we have to start getting you prepared for that. You have etiquette down, but now you need a leadership course, you need to see and understand our assets and learn how to grow your own from what we have, the way Marcus and I have. There's so much to be done." He said.

"Do I have time? What if can't learn it all, what happens then?" I asked.

"Angel, calm down, I didn't mention any of this to make you panic. I just want you to be aware. You are not alone my Angel, I got you." he said.

"I just don't know if I can do this, and I'm starting to wonder if I even want to." I admitted.

"Well here are your answers right here, you can do this, and you don't have a choice. You are the bloodline, and being such, you have an obligation to keep this moving, and then to pass it on to the next heir which will be your child. It can be a burden, no doubt, but its also a family tradition. Without tradition, what are we?" He asked.

I turned my attention to the window and shook my head. Even though I've proven to myself time and time again that I am a survivor, this just seemed like it was too big for me. I knew that Deytwon would have my back, but I was supposed to be able to hold my own, the way he and Marcus were able to. The flag has to fly, not be bent and wrinkled at the corners.

"Angel, I know what you're feeling, believe me, its the same way Marcus and I felt when the torch was passed to us. We weren't sure that we could handle it either. Our father's made it look so easy, but it wasn't, but you know what, its not impossible, and that's all you need to remember." He said

I looked over at him and nodded my head.

"Do you believe that I can handle this?" I asked.

"I know you can." He replied with a smile.

"Then I will give it my all." I said feeling a bit more confident that Deytwon had such faith in me.

When the plane landed we were let off and escorted to a limo that had been waiting on us. Once inside Deytwon took my hand and kissed it. I leaned back on him and brought his arms around me.

"I love you." I whispered.

"I love you." He whispered back.

About thirty minutes later we pulled up to an extremely tall building, whose top was hard to see.

"What in the world?" I asked as we stepped out of the limo.

"Thanks man." I heard Deytwon said just before closing the door.

"The Empire State Building." I said reading the sign.

"You ready?" he asked.

"What? But its closed." I said as he took my hand.

"Not for us." He replied as we walked over to the building.

"Welcome Mr. Richards, its a honor to have you visiting us this fine morning." Said a man as he opened the door for us to enter.

"The pleasure is mine." Deytwon said as he shook hands with the man.

"Right this way sir, madam." Another man said as we entered the building.

We followed him over to the elevator where he waited for us to step in before he followed suit.

Once inside he pressed the button and we went up.

"Everything is ready?" Deytwon asked the man.

"Yes sir, everything is as you've requested sir." The man said turning to face Deytwon.

"Wonderful." Deytwon said.

The elevator rose to the eightieth floor, then we got off and rode six more flights.

"Yeah ready?" He asked giving my hand a gentle squeeze as the doors started to open.

"Yes." I replied

When the doors opened we stepped off of the elevator. There was a path of lights and rose petals on the floor leading to a place outside.

"Deytwon, this is... oh my gawd." I said as I brought my hands to my face once we were out on a deck like area. The rose petals and lights led up to a candle lit dinner sitting on top of a table that was decorated with a white cloth and more rose petals that look as though they had fallen from the two large bouquet of roses sitting on the table.

That's when I heard the melody of "I am you're Angel", which was one of my favorite songs being played, and my favorite signer of all time stepped out of the shadows singing his song. The original song was a duet but he was still killing it.

"OH MY GAWD!! OH MY GAWD!" I screamed jumping up and down.

I looked over at Deytwon who was smiling and laughing at me. I had become so emotional that I started to cry. I couldn't believe it, I was getting a private concert with my favorite singer, singing my favorite song.

Deytwon walked over to me and touched my arm to guide me over to the table to have a seat. I instead turned and put my arms around him.

"I so love you." I said looking up into his eyes. He smiled and wiped my eyes.

"I am so glad, because I've been so waiting so long to hear you say those words to me. He said.

"I've waited longer for you to come into my life. You are my dream, and I stopped believing that it would happen. I stopped believing that I deserved it because of all the bad decisions that I've been making. But you are here, and you love me." I said still crying.

"And I always will." He said as he wiped my tears before bending down on one knee

"Angel, from the moment I first laid eyes on you, I knew that you were to be my wife, and I would be honored if you would allow me to spend the rest of my life, showing you why." He said.

I looked down at him on one knee and I cried harder. I loved him so much, so fast in such little time, I knew that it had to be something more than coincidence, I knew that it was fate and I knew that he was where I wanted and needed to be.

"Yes, yes Deytwon, I will marry you. Every day for the rest of my life!" I said crying.

Deytwon slipped a huge diamond ring onto my finer, then he jumped up on his feet and twirled me around as my favorite singer began to sing his song titled 'Forever'.

When we let go he turned around to the railing and shouted down towards the street.

"SHE SAID YES!!!"

I turned him around and cupped his face as I pulled him into a deep passionate kiss.

I loved him and he loved me, and I knew that in my heart without a shadow of a doubt that we would have this guarantee for the rest of our lives.

****

## Chapter 19

### Deytwon

"Yo?" Marcus asked answering the phone.

"What's good homie, where are you these days, its hard to catch up with you." I said before taking a pull of my cigar.

"I mean, you know me, I'm everywhere? Why what's good?" He asked.

"So I talked to Tiff, she said there was this weird ass smell in your house.." I started but he cut me off.

"Fuck you mean you was talking' to my wife?" He demanded to know.

"Dog, hear me, she said there was this weird ass smell in your house, so I told her don't trip, its probably nothing." I said.

"Fuck you do man?" Marcus asked with as sigh after a few seconds of silence.

"Nah, I just shot her a text to meet you where you are now. She made it out." I replied then I hung up the phone.

I sat back and continued to enjoy my cigar and brandy as I watched the gray and black smoke from his house dominate the sky over what used to be his American dream house.

Payback for stepping foot on *my* property and a small indication of how unprotected he leaves his wife. While *he* is off limits, *she* is not.

I'd have to get him back later for blowing up my car. In the mean time I had to get Angel ready for the coronation, and keep her in hiding. It wasn't enough that she was now my fiancee, she needed to be crowned in order to keep her protected.

I had to chuckle at the irony, the same organization started to strengthen the bond of brotherhood was now the same organization harboring a battle against its own creed.

Maybe something like this was going on years ago, and that's what made Angel's great grandfather fall back from keeping his leadership position.

I did feel bad because all my life my father, grand father and great grandfather taught me that the Big Boys represented honor, and prestige. They prided themselves on standing up for and doing what was right, over doing what was easy. They gave me the foundation to stand on, yet here Marcus and I were crumbling it up.

"Ahh well." I said with a shrug as I stood to my feet to stretch.

That nigga got to learn, don't fuck with me and mine, if you want to keep you and yours. That was the Deytwon Richards Creed.

### Marcus

"Baby, soon as I got to the car, the house exploded! It was crazy, I could've died!" My wife said crying in my arms. I had been chilling' with Gia, my 'go to girl' in my row-house on Capitol Hill, when I got the call from Deytwon about Tiff.  No sooner had I rushed Gia out of the house did Tiffani pull up in her Lexus, frantic as hell.

Thank God she didn't see Gia hop the fence into my neighbors yard. Luckily she was too crazed to notice.

"yeah baby girl, I know, I'm so sorry I wasn't there to protect you." I said in my most loving husband voice. Although I did really love Tiffani, my thoughts were on Deytwon and his fuckin' nerve.

I was pissed how this nigga came after my wife, off that bullshit with a bitch that he knew I fucked. He knew I slutted Angel's ass out, and she *let* me. Yet he took sides with her over me, his brother. It wasn't like I was letting the car explode on his property, the timer was set perfectly.

"Baby, your heart is racing are you OK?" Tiff asked as she sat up and looked at me. She placed her hands on both sides of my face to get me to focus on her. I watched the tears stream down her face an on to her cheeks. The hurt in her eyes almost pierced through my anger, but I didn't want to release the fire I felt over this shit with Deytwon just yet. I tend to plot best when I'm heated.

"Baby girl, I almost lost you, *of course* I'm not OK" I said pulling her in close to me.

"Oh Marcus.." She mumbles as she continued to cry.

Seconds later I heard a knock on the door. Shocked, I looked over wondering who it could be. Very few knew about this house, and *they* knew not to come over uninvited.

"Hold on baby, let me go get the door." I said as I slipped out from underneath her.

I walked over to the picture window and peered out to see a black Bentley with an American flag and a Big Boys flag on it, parked in front of my house, and an unmarked fed car parked in front of it with the flashers on.

I opened the door before a secret agent looking nigga could knock again.

"Sir, are you Mr. Marcus Jones?" The man who was standing in front of a woman that I couldn't quite see, asked.

"yeah." I replied with a shrug.

"You have a special delivery sir." He said as he stepped aside to reveal Mimi our messenger. She only came out when there was a big announcement, or a big invitation. My heart always pumped when I saw her because it could mean that my father or one of my grandfathers had passed.

"Mr. Jones, you're looking well." She said as she bowed her head towards me.

"What's going on Mimi?" I asked needing her to get to the point.

"I have an invitation for you sir." She replied pulling a black envelope out of her bag.

I took it and looked it over. My name was the only thing written across the front. I looked back up at Mimi who wore a worried look across her face, and I knew why. She was required to get my fingerprint to confirm that I received the message. If she didn't, she would be punished severely. I used to give her a hard time until she did whatever it was that I wanted a the time.

"Sir, will you please confirm that you've received this?" She asked in a humbled tone.

Ignoring her I opened the letter and damn near had a heart attack as I read the words.

*Mr. Marcus Jones*

*May this letter find you in the best of spirits. We have some great news to share with you that brought joy to our hearts immediately. For fifty years the Big Boys have been forced to operate as an incomplete unit as we lacked our 3$^{rd}$ Heir. Now, we are pleased to announce that the 3$^{rd}$ heir has been discovered and confirmed!*

*Angel Powers of the Powers blood line has been confirmed as the 3$^{rd}$ heir and will take her place as the 3$^{rd}$ leader via a Coronation Ceremony that will take place, one month from today.*

*As a current leader of the Big Boys, your presence is required as you will be presenting at the ceremony. Let us all rejoice as the Big Boys will once again be a complete unit!*

*-Big Boys -Elders*


I dropped the letter from my hands as anger and I were becoming one.

"That bitch *survived*?!" I mumbled to myself. I couldn't believe she survived the explosion.

*'I watched that car blow high into the sky, there's no way she could've survived that, unless, she wasn't in the car.. but then how?'* I thought to myself as I became angrier by the minute.

"Excuse me, Mr. Jones, may I please have your thumb print for confirmation?" Mimi's soft voice brought me out of my trance.

I looked over at her with fire in my eyes, although it wasn't at her, she was in the line of it for grabbing my attention in such a critical time.

"*Please* Mr. Jones, you know what they will do if I don't get your thumb print. As always, I will do *anything*." She begged.

*'Hmm, I could use some head right about now.'* I thought as I raised my eyebrow just as my

wife walked into the foyer.

"Baby, I don't remember this house." She said startling me. I damn near forgot that she was here. I was about to be all the way fucked up.

*'Shit, the fuck is everything going wrong now for?!'* I thought to myself as I snatched the clipboard from Mimi. I quickly ran my thumb across the ink before pressing it onto the slip under my name. At the top of the paper was Deytwon's name and thumb print also.

"You've already been to see him, huh." I said shoving the clipboard back at her.

"Yes, he's the one who said you'd be here. Thank you." She said before bowing her head and walking off.

*'That bitchass nigga set this whole shit up!'* I shouted within myself.

I slammed the door behind her and turned around bumping into my wife who was close enough to tell me what color my tonsils were.

"Not now baby." I said walking passed her.

"Was that a message from the Big Boys?" She asked.

"yeah." I replied pouring myself a drink.

"Was it about your dad, or one of your granddads, is everything OK?" She asked sounding concerned.

"Everything is fine." I replied firmly.

"You dropped your letter baby." She said walking over to the door to pick it up off the floor.

"Oh, so I did." I replied before taking a sip.

"You want me to read it to you?" She asked.

"I already read it." I answered dryly.

"Oh, *bad* news?" She asked as she folded it and put it back into the envelope.

"Great news, they found the 3<sup>rd</sup> heir." I said as I looked around for my keys.

"Oh baby, that's so wonderful! Are you guys excited?!" She asked perking up.

"Giddy as a school girl. You seen my keys?" I asked turning over couch cushions.

"Am I missing something here?" She asked.

"Huh?" I asked looking over at her. I was only half listening to her.

"Why aren't you excited about finding the 3<sup>rd</sup> heir? You guys haven't had your 3<sup>rd</sup> heir in fifty years." She said.

"I mean, what is it that you want me to do Tiff, jump up in the air and click my heels together? Run around the house in a circle singing cume bye ya? I'm happy, I just got other things on my mind. Can *I* be most important, *sometimes*?" I asked flipping the script.

"Baby you are most important to me all the time." She said as she walked over and put her arms around me.

"Good, because right now, this right here, is what I need. Just me and you." I said lying as I kissed her lips.

"You got it baby!" She smiled as she jingled my keys in the air,

I took them from her and grabbed her hand and walked towards the door.

"Baby, where are we going? Our next closes house is in Connecticut." She said as we headed out of the door.

"Well, if its alright with you baby girl, I need to just get away for a lil bit." I said as I locked up the house.

"Where did you have in mind?" She asked.

"Paris." I replied as I took her hips and walked her down the steps.

191

## Chapter 20

### Deytwon

"Its been a long time since we've all been in the same location all at once. This would be a good opportunity for a crazy nigga to wipe the Big Boy Leadership out." Marcus said as we sat in the largest lounge room in the Big Boy Mansion on Big Boy island. We were playing the game system while waiting for the elders to arrive.

I just looked at him and shook my head.

"*This* the shit that goes through *your* mind." I asked.

"yeah, believe it or not, the world ain't rosey. But I guess you can't tell a man in love *that* shit, huh?" He asked with a chuckle.

"*You* wouldn't know?" I asked.

"Not on the level you seem to." He said chuckling again.

"I'm good, never worry, I go in good, I come out better. Bet it." I said.

"Hey, you ain't gotta prove shit to me. I ain't above or beneath you." He said as he stood an walked over to the bar to pour himself a drink.

"So let me ask you this, did you know that there are missiles in tunnels underwater that accept codes. So if aircraft, or ships try to come close to this island without permission they will be attacked? That's why we always have to give that info when we change planes or boats." I said.

"Nah, my dad ain't never told me that." He said shocked.

"Do you ever ask them questions?" I asked wondering how he didn't find learning about this island and everything Big Boy, didn't fascinate him.

"Ask for what?" He asked

"Because it takes more than having power, to be powerful." I said.

"Here you go. Man, we're in the prime of our lives. We got all the money, all the houses, all the cars fifty niggas could have comfortably. You used to be a wild boy, wilder than me. How you get so serious, what happened man?" He asked.

"A lot actually. My lifestyle was catching' up to me and almost took me out." I replied thinking back to my last motorcycle accident.

"So you just went from a thousand to zero." He asked.

"Never, zero means you have nothing. I have everything. I'm good." I said.

"Even being that I was way more chill than you, *I* was labeled the bad boy." Marcus said with a chuckle.

"Because you always got something up your sleeve. Marcus, the master manipulator. But me, I was always flat out, it is what it is, take it or leave it." I replied.

"So I'm just a sleaze ball ass nigga is what you saying'?" Marcus asked.

"Nah that's what *you* saying'." I replied.

"Fuck that shit. Look here, there's always a method to my madness. I don't do shit that don't come with a benefit." He said.

"A benefit for who?" I asked.

"For me nigga, what the fuck." He said with a chuckle.

"Master Manipulator." I replied with a chuckle of my own.

"Sleaze ball ass nigga." He added

"You'll be that, huh." I said with a chuckle

"I'll be that. Fuck I care what people think?" He asked.

"True." I replied.

"Excuse me, the Elders have arrived." Said Gertie, chief of staff at the Big Boy mansion.

"Damn, I ain't even hear the plane come in." Marcus said as he and I headed outside to meet our fathers and grandfathers.

When we got out there we saw a helicopter and a plane up on the hill, and two yachts being docked.

Marcus and I walked over to the leadership garden that overlooked the island and the ocean. Only Big Boy leaders and official gardeners were allowed in. If you ever wondered what the garden of Eden must've looked like, I'm certain you pictured this garden.

"Man, I haven't seen my father or grandfather's in years." Marcus said shaking his head.

"Me either." I replied feeling bad how I allowed my life to neglect my parents.

Marcus and I stood near the entry door away from the table in the middle of the garden. We learned that because we are the leaders, if we are sitting at the table, no one can enter until we got up from the table.

The last time we all met up on the island, we had our father's and grandfathers waiting outside of the garden for an hour due to our ignorance. That's why I never hesitate to ask questions, big or small.

We watched our fathers being escorted towards us by Big Boy guards. They brought them to the door, saluted Marcus and I, then stepped to the side to allow our father's to walk through.

"Whoa old man, almost didn't recognize you there!" Marcus said as he and his dad embraced.

"You should learn to recognize me well, I am you in 23 years." His father joked.

"Pop!" I said embracing my own dad.

194

"My son. It has been too long." My father said.

"Indeed it has. Granddad, you're looking well." I said as I braced my grandfather.

"Richard genes my boy, Richard genes!" He said.

"No doubt about that." I said.

"Great-granddad, how are you?" I asked embracing him next.

"All is well my son." He said.

"Well, we have important business to discuss. This coronation ceremony is one of great significance. It will therefore be like no other." My great-grandfather began.

"You two, Marcus and Deytwon, current leaders, will be presenting the ring and the crown to Heiress Angel Powers, of the Powers Bloodline." Marcus' great grandfather added.

"With Heiress Angel being the first female heir, the world will look at us differently. No respect will be lost, but with a Queen in place of what was once a Kings chair, they will have questions." Marcus Grandfather said.

"As long as you three present a united front, no one will ever question our empire." My grandfather said.

Marcus and I shared a knowing glance.

## Marcus

After the meeting I went out to the beach where I saw my great grandfather wading in the shallow part of the water. He was skipping rocks across, watching until they stopped bouncing against the waves before he'd toss another.

"Sir." I said after approaching him.

"I used to love to skip rocks across the water as a boy, some things never get old." My great grandfather said as he skipped another rock.

"Seems more like a thinking strategy." I said.

"That's because you're a thinker, a strategist. Not everything in life requires much thought. Sometimes you're just damned if you do or your just damned if you don't." He said dusting his hands after throwing his last rock.

"What are we discussing here?" I asked.

"Patience is still a virtue, *no?*" He asked implying that I was rushing him.

"Patience requires time, time is money." I answered.

"And wisdom outlasts them both." He said stepping out of the water.

"Check." I replied with a head nod.

"So who's this girl and where did y'all find her?" He asked as we started walking along the beach.

"Her name is Angel Powers, she was born and raised in Washington, DC. We hired a private detective to find her." I said.

"Why?" He asked.

"Why not, someone from the Powers bloodline would've surfaced anyway. Shouldn't we be in control of the how and when?" I asked.

"And so you brought Deytwon in on it? He asked.

"How can I make a leadership move without him?" I asked back only half telling the truth.

"Leaders don't ask for permission, they simply lead." He said.

"And then what, spring her on him to accept?" I asked.

"He would've never known about her in the first place." He said.

I looked over at him confused.

"Explain." I said wanting to know if he was saying what I thought he was saying.

"My son, answer me this. Who holds the greater shares of Big Boy assets?" He asked.

"The Powers bloodline" I answered.

"Who then will have equal assets should the Powers bloodline cease to exist?" He asked.

"Jones and Richards." I said

"Exactly, so then are you trying to undo what has been done?" He asked.

"As long as they breathe they have entitlement." I said playing devil's advocate,

"Yes, as long as she breathes, *her* entitlement will be over *you*." He explained.

"Deytwon is set to marry her." I said.

"Yes, my first wife died of cancer." My great grandfather said unphased.

"So what should I do, adviser?" I asked with a chuckle.

"You're a thinking man, think.. if they join forces, they will become one in Power. The Jones's will have a seat at the table, but we won't have much to eat." He said as we stopped walking.

"I see." I said.

"Rumor has it, Cecil Powers walked away, but what man would walk away from all of this?" He asked holding his arms out towards the sky.

"I already know that he didn't walk away." I said.

"And if you're smart, you'll know that she didn't walk away either." He said with a wink.

I shook my head and smiled.

*****

## Chapter 21

Angel

One month later..

I sat in a big beautiful room overlooking a blue ocean and up above a blue sunny sky. The grass was neatly groomed, decorated with a large garden which displayed an array of beautiful colors. The entire scene all came together to look like paradise. It was like no place that I have ever seen, not even TV could capture something this gorgeous.

I nervously sat in a chair while five women worked on my appearance. One did my toes, the another worked on my hands, another was doing my hair, another did my make up and the sixth woman smoothed lotion over my body. I felt like a queen as I was being prepped for my big day. Today was the day of my coronation. Deytwon worked very hard to whip me into mental shape for this big event. In nearly a years time he stuffed me with information that would benefit me mentally, physically, emotionally and even spiritually. I knew that even with all that I did know, I still had a lot to learn, but I was confident that I would learn it all in due time.

After the day Marcus tried to kill me, we had no more incidents with him. I don't know if it were because he believed he succeeded or if he knew that I finally realized who I was. Deytwon said that although I had not had my coronation, the fact that I knew that I was the heir would be enough to have Marcus punished. However, I didn't want that, yes, I was angry at him for trying to kill me, and for treating me like shit, but I was wrong too. Knowing that he was married and choosing to be with him anyway, is the reason karma was coming for me so strongly, at least that's what it was in my eyes.

Nevertheless, I just wanted to spend the rest of my life being happy, being in love with the man that I've waited my whole life for. As far as I was concerned, Marcus was a non-factor when it came to anything that was of significant importance to me, and power wasn't one of those things, at all.

When the ladies were done working on me, another woman walked in with my gown. It was a long white gown studded with diamonds, and it was absolutely gorgeous.

I stood to my feet as the other ladies all ooh'd and aww'd at the gown. I took it and walked over to the mirror where I held it up against me.

"This is so beautiful, I have never seen a dress this fabulous." I said as I watched the diamonds reflect the lights in the room.

"Lets get you dressed, they will be starting soon." Said the woman who brought the dress out to me. I looked over at her and smiled. I wished that my grandmother was there to be with me in this very special moment in my life. She always told me that I was meant for great things, it would've been nice for her to see the manifestation of her confession.

The woman helped me ease into the gown, then she zipped me up and turned me towards the mirror. A single untamed tear fell from my eyes as I took it all in. The dress fit me well, and I felt like Queen.

"These are your shoes, they are made of Crystal." The woman said as she took my shoes off of a pillow and sat them on the floor before me.

"They wont break on me, will they?" I asked looking down at the beautiful shoes.

"No, these are very strong, good quality. Try them on, they should fit you very well." The woman said.

I stepped into the shoes to find that the woman was correct, they did fit me well, not only that, for heels, they were very comfortable.

"Now, lets have a look at you." She said turning me towards the mirror.

"Oh my!" I said looking at myself from head to toe for the first time since having the dress on. I barely recognized myself.

"You are now ready, and they are ready for you." The woman said smiling at me in the mirror.

"Thank you." I said smiling back at her.

I was escorted out of the room, through the house, and out to the beautifully decorated yard. I stepped outside and walked on a long white carpet that lead towards a platform.

There was a fleet of helicopters, jets and planes on a field to the left of everything. On the right were many Yachts docked at the shore. The island itself was beautiful and the crystal clear waters added wonderfully to the scenery. I looked straight ahead, and that's when I noticed the crowd of people. I was taken aback at how many people had actually come out for this.

When everyone saw me coming they all stood to their feet. Deytwon and Marcus were standing on the platform dressed in white suits with diamond crowns on their heads. Behind them were two older men who looked just like each of them. They too were wearing crowns and there were two more elderly looking men also wearing crowns, but they were still seated.

The crowd was very large, everyone smiling and watching me as I approached the platform. I was excited and nervous all at the same time. Never have I felt this important in my entire life, except for whenever I was with Deytwon.

When my eyes met Deytwon's they locked and suddenly I felt that everything was OK He smiled and winked at me which caused me to smile and blush.

I was escorted to a seat in the center of the platform where I was as to have a seat. Everyone was silenced as the eldest men who had still been seated made their way over to me. I stood to my feet as they approached me, which caused them to laugh.

"Good Afternoon young lady. I am Arthur Jones, the Father of Marcus Jones I and grandfather of Marcus Jones II. I knew your great great grandfather Cecil Powers Jr. when I was a young child. He was a great man, and I am honored to meet his off spring today. You are the first woman to wear the crown, you are single-handedly bringing The Big Boys brotherhood into a new era. This is good, anything that does not adapt will die. I lie the responsibility of adaptation of the Big Boys on you. Never fail to adapt to the changes of the world, but never succumb to anything that will not promote growth" Mr. Arthur said to me as he rubbed my head with some kind of oil. Then he took a step back.

"Good Afternoon, I am Douglas Richards, Father of Douglas Richards II and grand father of Deytwon Richards. I too knew your great great grandfather when I was just a young boy. I agree that he was a great man, and I can see that his blood runs strong in your veins. You may not understand the keen significance of your presences here today. You are the continuation of your bloodline. You will pick up the torch and carry it for your family. It is up to you to educate your off spring on the significance of the Big Boy Brotherhood and why that as long as the blood line breathes, the brotherhood should always be alive. This responsibility, I lie upon you." Deytwon's grandfather said as he rubbed my head with a different oil.

Then the two elders bowed to me and walked back to their seats. That's when the two men behind Deytwon and Marcus walked over to me.

"Good Afternoon, I am Marcus Jones I, the father of Marcus Jones II. I never had the pleasure of meeting your great great grandfather, but I have heard marvelous stories about him. He upheld the vision and creed for the Big Boys Brotherhood, and I lie on you the responsibility to do the same. Learn and teach what It means so that the lessons will be proudly passed down through the generations to come." Marcus' father said as he placed oil my head. Then he stepped back.

"Good Afternoon, I am Douglas Richards II father of Deytwon Richards. I have never met your great great grandfather, but he was spoken very highly of. He helped pioneer many acts of kindness and brotherhood. I lie on you the same responsibility to ensure that The Big Boys are always known for their good works." Deytwon's father said as he placed oil on my head.

"Welcome to the family my dear." He added with a wink before taking the step back. Then they bowed their head to me before walking back to their seats, signally that it was time for Deytwon and Marcus to step forward.

I watched Deytwon walk over with the proud look on his face. He couldn't suppress his smile if he wanted to, and I sure didn't want him to, it was the thing that kept me comforted.

"I am Deytwon Richards, I am here to present you with the Big Boys ring. This is a symbol of our brotherhood and it is recognized through out the world as a symbol of Power, Strength, Courage, and Brotherhood. The three diamonds represent the three founding fathers of the Big Boy Brotherhood. When this is placed on your finger you will from there after have the responsibility of upholding the Big Boy creed." Deytwon said as he took my hand and slipped the ring onto my finger. Then he stepped back and turned his attention to Marcus.

Marcus stepped up with the crown in his hand. He walked directly in front of me and looked me in the eye.

"This is the crown that we wear to represent the royalty that runs in our veins. Wear this crown with your head high as one who understand all that it represents." Marcus said dryly as he put the crown on my head. I smiled at him before he walked back over to Deytwon who was smiling as though he knew what my smile meant. Then they bowed their heads and walked away.

"Come, we will now have the lighting of the candles." Marcus' great grandfather said. They all walked over to the stand of candles that sat on my right side. One by one they lit the candles saving the one in the middle for me.

I walked over and took the lighter from Deytwon and lit the candle that represented me.

"The final candle has been lit, and now the Big Boy Coronation Ceremony is complete. This ceremony is of utmost importance because for the fist time in 50 years we have our third bloodline member in ranks and now we once again a complete unit." Marcus' great grandfather said.

"All hail Queen Angel of the Powers bloodline." Marcus's great grandfather said.

The crowd in the audience all bowed and the members on the platform raised their rings in the air.

Once the ceremony was completed everyone met up at the reception which was set up in the courtyard area of the mansion. I was seated at the head table next to Deytwon and Marcus. The fathers and grandfathers sat at tables behind us as a show of support. The three of us were the current leaders and the fathers and grandfathers were the Elders, they stepped down and allowed Deytwon and Marcus to have control and took on the role as advisers.

Everyone came to the tables, spoke to the elders, then spoke to us. Once all of the congratulations were done the music started and the food was served. The food was made to order by Master Chefs from across the globe, everything was wonderful.

"So how you holding up?" Deytwon whispered to me once we got a moment of peace.

"I never imagined that it would be like this. This thing is bigger than I thought it would be." I said.

"Its even bigger than that, but you are doing well. The elders like you and they see a lot of

204

potential in you." He said.

"How can you tell?" I asked.

"Because there is no specific speech that they must give before crowning a person, they just speak. Everything that they've said to you was fruitful and with high expectation. They really seem to believe in you, your grandfather must've been some man." Deytwon explained.

"I wish I knew him." I said.

"We'll take a trip to the Big Boy museum, and you can learn about him there." Deytwon said taking my hand. I looked at him and smiled.

"You are so wonderful to me." I said as I lay my head on his shoulder.

"I'm in love with you, why wouldn't I be?" He asked. I snuggled up to him and slipped my fingers through his.

"I need a fuckin drink." I heard Marcus say as he stood up to leave the table.

"Baby, I'll be back." I said ready to follow him.

"Angel, do not push him, he already can not touch you, let him blow off his steam." Deytwon said taking my hand.

"Dey, I need you to trust me on this one." I said.

"Angel, do not make me get involved. I've known Marcus all of my life, I know what he is capable of." He said very seriously.

"So you're afraid for me?" I asked.

"No, I'm afraid of becoming someone that I cannot control, should something happen to you." Deytwon said.

"But you said that he cannot touch me." I reminded him.

"But why provoke him?" Deytwon asked.

I looked from Deytwon over to Marcus, he was standing at the bar having a drink when his wife walked over to him. He put his arms around her and handed her his cup to drink from. I turned my attention back towards Deytwon and nodded my head before sitting back in my seat.

"Just so you know, I wasn't looking for trouble." I said.

"I know, you just wanted to know why." He said.

"Yes, that's all." I said with a shrug.

"But I already told you why." Deytwon said.

"Power." I said looking up at him.

"Absolutely, it was never personal. Power is all he cares about, and is the basis for just about every move he makes. When you understand that, you kind of stop being mad at him and just start feeling sorry for him." Deytwon said before taking a sip of his drink.

"I hope that I never become that way." I said.

"You wont, because I'm going to fill your heart with something else." Deytwon said.

"Love." I replied blushing. He nodded his head then he moved in to kiss me.

****

## Chapter 22

### Deytwon

"I can't believe this man is getting married tonight." I said as I GQ'd in the mirror.

"*You*, can't believe it?" Came Marcus' sarcastic reply as he flipped through a car brochure.

"So you got any advice for me?" I asked as I smoothed a finger over my mustache.

"yeah, don't." He said flipping a page.

I turned around to look at him.

"Is that what I told *you*?" I asked reminding him of the support I offered to his nervousness the day he married Tiffany.

He looked up and shook his head before tossing the magazine to the side.

"This shit ain't just a lil awkward to you dog?" He asked leaning against the table.

"Fate don't wait for comfort." I said.

"So *this* was *fate*?" He asked sarcastically.

"Had to be, look what the fuck I'm 'bout to do, after the shit *you* did." I said.

"No doubt, so then I guess congrats man." He said as he extended his hand for me to shake.

"Thanks man" I said giving him a handshake hug.

"So we burying the hatchet?" He asked.

"We burning that bitch." I said turning back to look in the mirror.

"You think she'll let it go?" He asked.

"I know she will. My wife won't have time to worry about shit, especially about another nigga. I got plans for that woman." I said thinking about filling our lives with forever.

"I can dig it." He said just as my father stepped in the room.

"Everyone is in place, we're ready for you son." He said. I turned around to look at him.

"So, what you think Pop? How am I representing them Richards boys" I asked holding my arms out while giving a lil spin.

"Like a king." He said before giving me a hug.

"You look sharp dog." Marcus said added.

"Thanks man." I said as my dad adjusted my tie.

"You ready?" My dad asked.

"Never been more." I replied.

"Then lets do it." He said before turning to leave. Marcus followed him out. I looked up and smiled.

"Thank you for my queen" I said before following them out of the room.

◇◇◇◇

## Angel

That night, the sky seemed to be filled with the brightest stars. The moon was full and seemed so close as its reflection rippled along the waves in the water. The air was calm and the atmosphere was just perfect. The violinist played a melody that I fell in love with instantly upon hearing it. I never thought of having a midnight wedding, but this was turning out to be as beautiful as a daytime wedding.

"Girl, you look so beautiful." Salisha whispered as she escorted me down the aisle. Deytwon flew her and Anthony in just two hours before, which was around the time that the Coronation crowd began to dissipative.

We planned a small intimate ceremony with family and extremely close friends, Salisha and Anthony were the only two I invited as she was the only family that I really had.

"Thank you, Salisha, and I want to thank you for always being there for me. Giving me a place to stay when I was assed out, being my ear when I needed someone to talk to, and giving me all the advice that I didn't want to hear. I love you like a sister." I said.

"I love you too, and you are my sister, and I always got your back." She said giving my arm a gentle squeeze.

I smiled as I allowed her words to warm my heart, it couldn't have received them better if they had come from my grandmother herself.

As we got closer down the aisle everyone stood to their feet and turned their attention towards us. Deytwon broke into a wide cheesing smile, while Marcus stood there wielding a fake smile. The Father's and Grandfathers all seemed genuinely happy as they too wore smiles that seemed to match that of Deytwon's.

Then suddenly the melody changed and we heard a song that took my heart the very first time I heard it years ago, and what's more, the actual singers were there to perform it.

"GIRL, NO HE DIDNT GET THEM!!" Salisha exclaimed as we heard 'All my Life" being sang.

I looked up at Deytwon who was looking at me with the sexiest look he could possibly muster. Then he mouthed the words 'I love you.'

"I love you too." I said as tears came to my eyes.

When I approached him he buried his eyes into my own and wiped the tears from them.

"I told you, only happy tears, from here on out." He whispered to me.

The duo brought the song down to a soft hum as the Pastor stepped over and in front of Deytwon and I.

After Salisha confessed that she was the one who was giving me away, Deytwon and I stood in front of one another holding hands. I barely heard anything the Pastor said because I was to busy falling in love with this man over and over again as I watch tears escape his eyes as well. We basically took turns wiping tears away and laughing at each other for doing so.

We exchanged the rings and repeated the vows as they were told to us by the Pastor. Then we were granted permission to kiss. Deytwon lift my veil and leaned in to give me the sweetest kiss I had ever experienced.

"I now give you, Mr. and Mrs. Deytwon Richards!" The pastor shouted.

All of the Big Boys raised their rings in the air while the others in the crowd clapped and cheered. Seconds later a display of fireworks were set off in the distance.

"This was all so beautiful, this whole day was like moments in paradise." I said as Deytwon carried me through the well wishers.

"And just think, our lives are only just beginning. But that bouquet, you can get rid of that, we wont be coming back here." He said.

I looked down at the beautiful assortment of flowers, smiled, and tossed it behind us.

"Good, because I don't want to even look back, I only want to move forward, with you." I said before kissing him.

From that very moment, all of the emptiness, sadness, feeling of insignificance and neglect had all been wiped clean from my spirit, and I was completely ready to start the next chapter of my life, with the man who had become the love of my life.

## Marcus

I stood there with my hands stuffed in my pockets as we watched Deytwon and Angel take off in his jet. It was interesting to watch them interact with one another. It was almost like love illuminated off their connection. In some ways I was actually happy for Deytwon, he waited a long time for a wife. He turned down many perfect potential women just to wife a hoe. But like they say, one man's trash is another man's treasure. I mean, I guess it is what it is.

I did everything I could to deter him from wanting her, outside of knocking that bitch up, but he wasn't hearing me over his heart. I didn't even know love came that real, and for damn sure didn't want to find out. While I do love my wife, if she left me, most of my sadness would be for show.

"The ceremony was so beautiful. She was such a beautiful bride." My wife said as she linked her arm around mine.

"yeah, it was very nice." I lied, I hated every second of it.

"So have you met her, is she nice?" My wife asked.

"I mean she cool. I don't know her all like that." I said with a shrug.

"What's the matter baby?" She asked as she slipped both arms around my body.

"I'm good baby, it's after midnight, I'm just a lil sleepy." I lied.

"yeah, speaking of sleep, are we going home tonight?" She asked.

"I figured we could just got to the vacation house in the Bahamas, you ready?" I asked as I moved out of her embrace and took her hand.

"Oh yeah!" She exclaimed.

"Aright, let me go say good night to the elders. I'll be right back." I said while walking away.

"Good night gentlemen, the wife and I are off." I said after I approached them. They all stood to greet me.

I shook the Richards' hand and hugged my father and grandfathers before stepping off.

"Marcus, a word please." My grandfather said

"OK" I replied.

We walked a little ways away before he spoke his peace.

"Your great grandfather shared with me about the conversation you two had earlier." He started once we were out of earshot of the rest.

"OK" I said.

"My advice on this is to give *them* some time to be married before any moves are made. Let him enjoy her. Right now she is still ignorant of her power. Only the Jones's have knowledge that the Powers have more power than *us* and the Richards." He said

'The longer we wait, the harder it will be." I said.

"Not necessarily, but I'll step out of your way as you make that call." He said.

"It will be handled." I said.

"Good night son." My grandfather said.

"Good night." I replied before rejoining my wife and together we boarded my jet.


~The End~

## Sneak Peak of The Big Boys Empire -Sidechick Blues Sequel

### by Nikida Bellezza

**Deytwon**

"How is she?" My mother asked the doctor after he rejoined us in the room.

He looked up from his pad and adjusted his glasses before speaking.

"Its not looking good. She is literally fighting for her life." He said softly as he touched my mom's arm.

I felt a tear escape my eye as my heart pumped with extreme heaviness. Before I realized it I was backing out of the room when my father caught my arm.

"Deytwon, please, your wife need you here, son." He pleaded, already knowing what I was going to do.

"I am here. I'm not the one fighting for my life." I said as more tears fell.

"Then be by her side. She can feel your presence." He said with ease.

"That's not good enough." I sneered as my heart filled with uncontrollable anger.

"Son, when the judgment is cast, I cannot save you." My fathers voice trembled when he spoke. I had never heard my father speak with anything more than sheer confidence and authority. But right now he sounded the equivalent to a man begging for mercy. The situation at hand was serious, my choice at this moment would either promote my life, or my death. I have never disobeyed my father before, and never intended too.

I looked over at my wife, who was struggling to meet the standards of the machines that she'd been hooked up to, to confirm that her life was still in tact. My heart felt like the life was being choked from it, and my eyes bled more warm tears. I turned to look at my father who seemed to grow smaller as my anger and hurt grew larger.

"I'm making a leadership move, step down." I spoke feeling like a man possessed.

My father stepped back and nodded his head surrendering to my authority.

Without saying another word I walked out of the room and took the freight elevator down to the garage where I got in my car and sped off.

Like a low jack, I knew exactly where to find the bitch who did this, and I did 80mph through red lights to my destination. Even though I was chased by several officers, I didn't care because I knew that once they got close enough to see my tags, they'd fall back, which they all did.

When I arrived at the house, I jumped out of the car and slammed the door closed with so much force it shattered the window. I walked up to the door and pulled out my gun to shoot the lock off, then I kicked it open to see Marcus in a chair carelessly hitting a jay.

"Dey, my man, what's good?" He asked off his chill shit.

I walked over to him and jacked him up out of the chair.

"Weak bitch! I know you called the hit on Angel!" I shouted.

"Hit? What hit my nigga?" He asked playing dumb.

I slammed him against the wall.

"I swear on your life, if she dies, you will die the same day." I growled as I felt love, compassion and reason drain from my heart.

"Dey, I ain't never seen you like this dog." He called behind me as I walked away.

Sidechick Blues The Plot by Nikida Bellezza

I ignored him as I opened the door.

"All this, over a bitch though? That's who we are? That's what we've become?" He shouted behind me.

I walked over to my car and kicked the glass out of my way.

"We brother's nigga! Always been, since birth, and this how it's gonna end?" He asked.

I looked over at him to see that he had a gun pointed at me.

"Do it. Fuck I got to live for without my wife!" I asked ready to die, but knowing that I wasn't about to. Marcus was a lot of things, but a killer wasn't one of them. oh he can plan it and pay for it, but he wasn't built to do it.

"She *will* die, those bullets were dipped in poison. I did that part myself. The genius part about it, It's untraceable. So they think she dying from the shots, but really it's the poison" He said with a chuckle.

I shook my head as I...


**The Big Boys Empire ~Sidechick Blues Sequel**


**--- COMING IN 2015**

**Questions / Comments / Concerns?  Connect with Author Nikida Bellezza via**

**Facebook: Nikida Bellezza**

**Instagram: @Nikida_Bellezza**

**Twitter: @NikidaBellezza**

**Good Reads: Nikida Bellezza**

**Thank You For Reading!!!**

**-Nikida Bellezza**

www.ingramcontent.com/pod-product-compliance
Lightning Source LLC
Chambersburg PA
CBHW070116260626
47160CB00004B/1490